I0822889

DRAGONBORN

THE BANNERET SERIES

2

JAMIE DALTON

Dragonborn

Cover Art by Grace Huart
Cover Typography and Copyright Magnetra's Design
Interior Design by AuthorTree

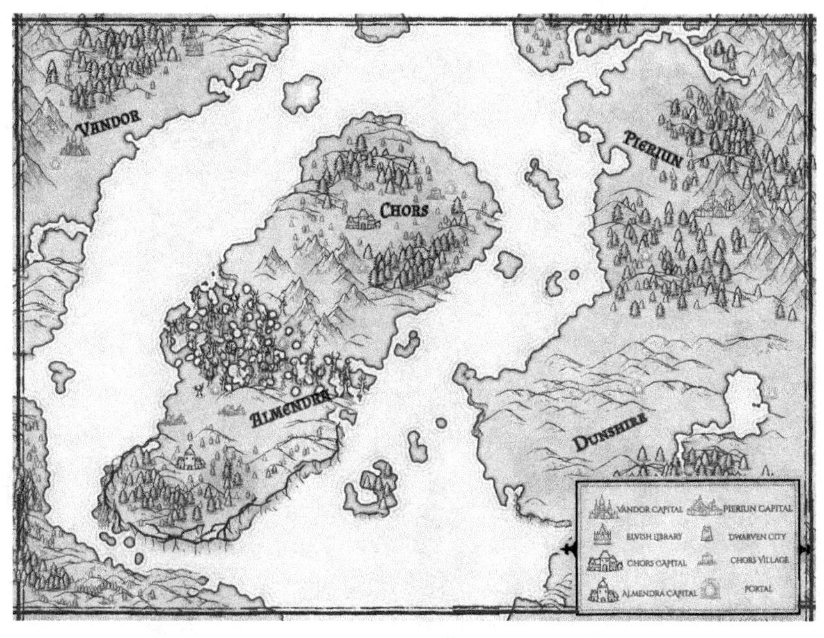
VANDOR
CHORS
PIERIUN
ALMENDRA
DUNSHIRE
VANDOR CAPITAL
PIERIUN CAPITAL
ELVISH LIBRARY
DWARVEN CITY
CHORS CAPITAL
CHORS VILLAGE
ALMENDRA CAPITAL
PORTAL

CHAPTER ONE

"None of you move."

Adalyn didn't dare swallow for fear of the blade at her throat reaching its mark. The portal had just closed behind her, and without being in physical contact with the rest of her party, she couldn't use her worldwalker ability to get them to safety. Her eyes shifted, and several more soldiers appeared in her peripheral vision from behind; she assumed they had hidden behind the portal.

The gruff voice startled her as it barked at the group again. "What business do you have in Chors? This is territory claimed by the king of Pieriun and any trespass… Venlian?"

"It took you long enough, Garret. Tell your men to lower their weapons." Her silver-haired elvish friend's demeanor shifted in a way she had never seen before. His stance commanded obedience without hesitation.

Garret sheathed his sword and nodded for his soldiers

to follow suit. “I didn’t expect to see you here. I thought you’d gone home.”

“I did. There’s a lot that we need to discuss. Did you recently take this territory?”

“Yes. The locals weren’t very resistant since their men are all gone. Mostly women and children, at this point.”

The faces of her friends in the village nearby flashed through Adalyn’s mind. “Were there many casualties?”

Garret eyed her with distrust. “What authority do you hold to ask me such questions?”

Venlian moved to stand next to her. “She is your superior and the leader of the Banneret.”

“Excuse me? That’s not possible. Glenda is…”

“Glenda is currently unable to fill the role. Is your camp nearby? This is going to be a long conversation.”

“It is.” Garret glanced past Vaeren and fixed his gaze on Nolan. Pointing towards his insignia, he asked, “Is he with you? I don’t recognize the mark.”

Adalyn took a step forward. “He is a member of my party.”

Garret’s eyes shifted from Venlian to Adalyn, noting the shift of power. “All right. If you will follow me, please.”

The group was escorted over a ridge that overlooked a valley with small hills protecting it. Rows of tents covered every inch of bare ground, and the buzz of chatter from the soldiers milling about carried on the wind.

“There’re so many of you,” Adalyn murmured.

“We’re one of the smaller units in Chors, but we get the job done. Around twenty thousand soldiers. And if you look over there,” Garret pointed towards a hill with a small number of blue-uniformed people milling about, "you'll see the Banneret troop stationed with us."

The thought that there were so many soldiers abandoned in Chors when the spell had frozen it in time had never occurred to Adalyn. She'd assumed that they had been recalled or killed.

This could change everything in Pieriun. These men would be returning to nothing. No homes, no jobs outside of the military, no families. The list of problems and opportunities for violence weighed on her heart.

Venlian's voice cut through her thoughts. "Is there somewhere private where we can chat? I'm afraid the news we have to share could be unsettling for your troops."

Garret led them towards one of the only physical structures in the encampment.

"What do you think happened to the previous occupants?" Nolan whispered to Adalyn as they entered a single-room cabin.

"I don't know if I want to know. We just have to remember that they still think we are at war. Technically, they *are* still at war. The rules of fair play are different for them right now." Adalyn whispered back.

Introductions were made and seats found for everyone before they began their tale. The color drained from Garret's face as their group filled him in on the past five hundred years of history.

"They're all gone. Everyone we knew is… gone." Silence filled the room as he processed what this meant not only for him, but for his soldiers. "What do we do? What are our orders, then?"

"Some of your men will be sent out to help recall

soldiers, while others will be returning. The records have been lost, so our king doesn't know how many troops to expect. Any information you can give us to help prepare would be appreciated. I will return and report before we send any of your soldiers home. They need to be told to not attack, only to hold a defense if provoked."

"Of course, that makes sense. I'm not sure how many soldiers are still in Chors. I know many were being recalled, but I didn't ask who stayed. Several of your Banneret have the ability to communicate with each other over vast distances and should be able to let you know better than I how many of us are left."

Adalyn nodded. "I will discuss it with them. Thank you."

Tears rimmed Garrett's eyes. "Is it… is it better?" he asked gravely. "Are we returning home to a good king?"

A reassuring smile spread across Venlian's face. "How good the kingdom will seem to you will depend on how well the soldiers behave when they return. I think things will be rough for a time, but you are returning to a kingdom at peace and a king who truly puts his people first. Our party is here to approach the king of Chors and request a truce."

Garret nodded, his eyes out of focus. "Yes, yes, that's good." With a start he looked up and locked eyes with Adalyn. "Be careful of the dragon, though. I've had reports of a dragon manipulating the war from behind the scenes. I don't know who it is, but keep an eye out."

Nolan shifted in his seat. "A dragon? They're real?"

"Very real and very dangerous. Your kingdoms will be

dealing with many things they have never encountered before. Dragons are one of the worst."

Adalyn was grateful Venlian agreed to accompany her to the group of Banneret. While it was good that Nolan and Vaeren stayed behind to answer Garret's questions, she really needed a face that these soldiers would recognize to help them trust her quickly. As the pair worked their way through the tents, the bandaged soldiers, dinged-up armor, and hint of iron in the air made her realize just how brutal this war had truly been. She had experienced a small part of it recently, but it clearly didn't compare to what her kingdom had gone through in the past.

The crowd parted as Venlian was recognized, making their way to the hill where the Banneret were set up easily accessible. A man dressed in blue with a red beard stretched an arm out towards Venlian.

"What brings you here, old friend? I heard you packed up and went home. Got bored away from the fight?"

Adalyn took a good look at the stranger. He was a giant of a man, the polar opposite of Venlian in every way—size, ears, nose, beard. His eyes were a deep, piercing green, and appeared to look into your very soul even as he continually took in his surroundings.

Venlian's face lit up with a smile that reached his eyes as he took the man's arm. "Not quite. It's good to see you, Brinn."

"And I, you."

Venlian let go and gestured towards Adalyn. "I would like you to meet Adalyn Mernt."

She stretched her hand in welcome, only for it to be left empty.

Brinn's eye took note of her leather britches and a blue coat similar to his, and fastened on the sword hanging at her waist.

"Before you say anything you may regret, let's find a place to talk." Venlian's voice rang with a tone of warning.

Brinn's eyes flashed as he turned around and waved for them to follow to a tent.

He didn't take their news much better than Garret did.

"This doesn't make sense."

Adalyn reached to place her hand on his arm in comfort but pulled it back as she reconsidered. "I know it's hard to believe. Your king went mad and made some very poor decisions. He sacrificed all of you, along with many others. King Coeus is not the same. We are here to try and fix this. We need the Bannerets' help, though. Garret mentioned that there were some here who could communicate with others in different troops."

Brinn only nodded.

Venlian spoke softly. "I think we need to call all of the Banneret in and have them assist in this. Only they can be fully told what happened until we report back to King Coeus. Can you bring them here?"

Brinn sat still for a moment before standing and silently leaving the tent.

Adalyn watched the flaps close behind him. "Is he going to be all right?"

"I'm not sure any of them will be in the short term. It will get better for some over time, but we're not prepared for this. I had no idea there were this many people left behind."

"They are returning to a new world entirely. So much has changed. I hope King Coeus and his council are creative, because this isn't going to have any simple solutions."

THE SHADOWS CAST BY CAMPFIRES RIPPLED ACROSS Adalyn's body as she worked her way through the soldiers towards the tents set up for her traveling party. While spending several days reporting and helping organize things in Pieriun for the returning soldiers, only a few hours had passed in Chors. She wasn't sure she would ever get used to the time difference between Chors and Pieriun from the living spell not being entirely broken. She figured that if it had been, her spirit friends would be at peace and no longer filling the tunnels between the dwarven settlement and the castle.

A familiar laugh carried over the chatter of the men she passed as she approached her own fire. She couldn't help but smile as she sat next to Nolan and watched Venlian talk with Garret in a more animated way than she had ever seen before.

"I didn't even know elves could laugh."

Nolan jumped at the sound of her voice. "How did you sneak up on me?"

She shot him a look as the smell of alcohol wafted her

way. "In your current state, a stampeding beast could sneak up on you. Where's Vaeren?"

"He's already sleeping it off." Nolan nudged her shoulder with his. "You know, this may be our last night of not having to stay on high alert. Relax a little."

She took the jug from his hand and brought it to her lips but didn't take a sip.

"How did it go back home?" Nolan slurred.

"Good. I let them know how many troops we estimate are still here and helped start organizing how to place them all. To be honest, I'm glad to be back. I'm not really cut out for figuring all of that sort of thing out."

Nolan grabbed the jug back and took another swig. "You don't give yourself enough credit. Wasn't Chef hoping to have you take over running the kitchen at the castle?"

She shot him a dirty look. "Don't mention that traitor."

Hands raised, Nolan leaned away from her and took another gulp.

Adalyn released a small sigh. "Sorry, I just feel like a lot has changed, and I'm not really sure I'm the right person for the job. Suddenly I'm in charge of the Banneret, whom I know basically nothing about. I have the king asking me my opinion on things, and to be completely honest, I would feel much better if I had been given this position for something other than the fact that I'm the only person he knew who had any magical abilities."

"Even with that, he wouldn't have given you the role if he didn't trust you."

She stared into the fire, deciding not to respond.

Nolan's fingers wove into hers. "You're not alone in this. You've got us. You've got me."

Looking into his eyes, she could see no hint of humor or lies. She squeezed his hand and smiled at him. "Thank you."

He smiled back as he raised the hand held in his and kissed it. "Never forget it."

"Will you two stop being so mushy over there?" Garret's voice snapped her attention away from Nolan, and Adalyn blushed as she dropped their still entwined hands between them. She looked over at the pair on the other side of the fire. Garret had a bottle in one hand and a goofy grin spread across his face, and Venlian was the stark opposite of his companion. She wondered what had caused the shift from his jovial self only moments before.

"That was a much quicker trip than I expected," Garret said, waving the bottle at Adalyn on its way up to his mouth.

"I'm sure with the time difference it felt much longer for her," Venlian responded without moving his gaze from her face.

Adalyn wondered if he had been drinking, as well. Maybe that could explain his odd behavior. "He's right. I was there four days. Everything is set up as much as it can be before you get there. King Coeus is expecting you, as is my second-in-command, Eridu. Since you will be the first army to return home, I highly suggest doing everything you can to assist the king. He will be looking for several people who both the returning troops and he can trust to help with the transition. I expect anyone deemed worthy of that will be well rewarded."

Garret's drunken grin told her that he understood exactly what Adalyn was saying.

Venlian stood and walked to her side, offering his hand to help her rise. "We should retire. With your return, I think we should begin our journey to the castle in the morning. Hopefully, we can arrive before another group of soldiers is sent to attack through the gates."

She took his hand and let her fingers slide out of Nolan's as she stood. "I agree. We should all get some sleep." Glancing between Nolan and the jug he held, she added, "It may be a good time to start sobering up, as well, or the journey will be miserable for some."

Nolan waved her off and mumbled something too quiet for her to hear as he rose and made his way to his tent. She wondered just how well her party would be holding up in the morning after the indulgent night they'd had.

CHAPTER TWO

"You all right back there, Nolan?" Gagging sounds from behind a tree on the side of the road confirmed Adalyn's suspicions.

Her very disheveled friend emerged and leaned on the tree to take a swig of water. "An early morning after a night of drinking is just cruel."

"You knew I was returning, as well as how quickly time passes over there compared to here. I'm surprised you didn't expect me to show sooner."

Nolan shot her a dirty look, but apparently decided it was better to not respond. After glancing at Vaeren, who sat on a log with his knees on his elbows as he shaded his eyes, he turned his attention towards Venlian. "Is that a smirk on your face? Do elves even smirk? I swear, you got around humans, and suddenly you're acting like one yourself."

"Just how, exactly, is an elf supposed to act?" Venlian asked with a raised brow, his smile remaining unchanged.

With a flourish of his hand, Nolan pushed off the tree

and circled in front of the group. "From what I've seen, you're all usually very poised, putting on airs and acting as if you know everything. Never something out of place, and the most delicate eaters I've ever seen."

Adalyn laughed at his over-the-top display. "You've never paid attention to how Venlian eats, have you?" Glancing over at the elf to see his reaction, she continued, "Delicate is not the word I would use to describe it."

A mask of emotion blanketed Venlian's face. She couldn't tell if he was amused or offended.

Turning from the group, Venlian began to walk away. "We should head out if we want to make it to the village by evening. Otherwise, we are sleeping under the stars tonight."

They spent most of the day in silence as they traversed through the woods. While Garret had assured them that they had cleared out the unnatural beasts from the area, everyone was on high alert. The memory of being attacked the last time they were here was still fresh in their minds.

Despite the occasional stops to accommodate Nolan's already emptied stomach, the group made good time. The sun created a mosaic pattern through the leaves on the path, the shadows shifting as the wind blew, and the noises of small animals surrounded them at all times.

By the time the sun cast a pinkish hue as it was setting, the village they'd previously visited had come into view.

"Do you think they will remember us?" Adalyn wondered.

"It's only been a handful of days for them. I would be more worried if they've forgotten us already," Venlian responded.

Nolan's stomach rumbled. "We're telling them everything, right? And who we really are?"

Adalyn nodded. "I think it's best. We're here to try and fix things, anyway."

"Did this place have an inn? I'm starving."

A familiar voice in the forest nearby made them all jump. "There's no inn, but if you're willing to explain to me what you meant about needing to tell us everything, I can guarantee a hot meal and warm place to sleep tonight."

"Bevin! I was hoping we would see you." Adalyn's face lit up and she walked over to greet her friend.

"Wait a minute, I'm serious. You know I need to protect everyone here. If you're not who you said you were, just who are you?"

"We're not from Chors," Venlian answered. "They're from Pieriun, but we are not here to attack. In fact, we come with an offer for a truce and are on our way to speak to your king. The world outside of Chors is not the same as it was a week ago for you."

"You're from Pieriun? *Are you kidding me?*" Bevin asked through gritted teeth as she drew her sword from its sheath. "You saw what the Pieriun army did to my village, and you have the nerve to come back here?"

"I promise we have no ill intention. I can show you the seal of our king with the letter we carry. The king you've been fighting is long dead. He did some horrible things, including casting a spell that sacrificed many people to trap your kingdom in time. It's been broken. We have no reason to be at war anymore. We are here on a mission to help set things right," Adalyn rushed to say, her hands held out in front of her.

"How do I know this isn't a lie?"

"I'm not sure there is anything that we could do that would help you believe us right now," Venlian acknowledged in a soothing tone. "You know of the large number of Pieriun troops sitting a day's walk away?"

Bevin nodded.

"They've already started leaving through the portal. We are recalling all troops from Chors. Soon you will see them passing by as they head towards the portal in even greater numbers. Feel free to send someone to confirm this if you must. We are willing to stay here if it will make you feel more comfortable."

Bevin's eyes glazed over for a moment as she processed what they had just said. She glanced around the party. "Where is Eridu?"

"She's back in Pieriun. She was needed to help with the return of our troops," Adalyn responded.

Bevin slowly nodded again and put her sword away. "I will send someone to check that what you say is true, but, strange as it is, I believe you. Don't say anything to anyone until I can confirm this myself. You're welcome to stay with us again, though, if you would like. The village women are still talking about the handsome men who passed through here not so long ago." With a wink, she turned and started towards the village while the others followed.

The blushing cheeks and hurried steps as the women and girls in the village came out to see them only proved that Bevin was entirely serious about the impact Nolan and Venlian had made on them. From some of the glances tossed their way, Adalyn speculated that Vaeren had caught a few eyes, as well.

"Mother, I brought visitors!" Bevin hollered as she opened the heavy wooden door to her home.

"Visitors! Who would possibly be... Oh, it's you!"

Adalyn's chest swelled with joy when she saw Bella stirring a giant pot over the fire as several of her children set the large table that ran down the center of the main room. "It's good to see you again."

"So soon! Of course you are welcome to stay for dinner. Do you need to stay the night, as well?"

"They will be staying a day or two while I look into something," Bevin said before the rest could speak.

Bella glanced back and forth between her daughter and the group in front of her, trying to read into just what her daughter meant. "Uh... of course. Why don't you all wash up. We're about to dig in."

With the tantalizing smell coming from that giant pot filling the room, they didn't have to be told twice.

"You wound me, sir! Why would you do something like that?"

Adalyn chuckled as she watched Nolan and Christian, one of Bevin's younger brothers, spar with sticks in the yard. Nolan dropped to the ground, holding the stick under his arm and groaning as he played out a very gruesome and drawn-out death.

"He's very good with kids, isn't he?" Bevin

commented, leaning against the wall of the house as she sat next to Adalyn.

"I guess he is."

Adalyn realized that she hadn't really seen Nolan much outside of preparing to take back the capital. Even before that, most of their interactions were his impromptu visits to the king's kitchen where she worked or in the training yard while she learned how to wield her sword.

"He is from a nomadic family, so I guess it shouldn't surprise me. His queen's caravan brings entire families, so there are usually children around."

Bevin nodded without removing her eyes from Nolan. A small smile formed as Christian reclaimed his sword and stabbed again. "I sent a few people to check on the gate and verify your story. They should be back tomorrow."

"Sounds good. We understand why you need to be cautious. I'm sorry that we lied to you before. We were just in a hurry with a very important mission for our king. We couldn't jeopardize that."

Adalyn tracked how Bevin was watching Nolan. Her stomach tightened as she recognized the look of interest in Bevin's eyes. While they had never become anything official, Adalyn considered Nolan much more than a friend. Images of his bare skin as they swam in the underground pool flashed in her mind. She could almost feel his touch on her again.

Bevin's voice disrupted her thoughts. "You say you are on your way to speak with my king. Does that mean that you are heading towards Trist?"

"It does."

"Could I travel with you? I've heard that they are

starting to recruit women, as well, if they are already fairly well trained." Bevin dropped her eyes to her fidgeting hands. "It's not safe for me to travel on my own."

Adalyn studied her friend's face for a moment. "You've already decided that we are telling the truth?"

Their eyes met. "I needed to send people to verify your story to protect my village. If I leave, I need to know that they will be safe. I do trust you, though."

"You do realize that we are trying to stop the war, right? There's a strong chance that they will no longer accept women into the ranks if that happens."

"I know, but I have to try. I can't be stuck here forever. There's got to be more out there for me than just… this," Bevin said, gesturing at the village.

A moment of silence passed between the two, neither one looking towards the sounds of Nolan dying yet again. This time his death was filled with cries about the biscuits that would never be eaten because of the travesty.

"All right. You can join us. We would appreciate a guide, anyway."

Bevins face lit up as she turned back to watch the battle in front of them. "Thank you. You have no idea what this means to me."

Nolan shook dirt from under his shirt and pulled grass from the collar of his leathers as the sparring session came to a close. A sturdy handshake between him and Christian, and the two walked over to join the women in the shade.

"You've trained your brother well, Bevin. He beat me more often than not."

Christian looked up at Nolan with a big grin on his face. "Of course I did! I'm the fiercest warrior our village has." He looked around as laughter erupted from the group, and Nolan rustled his hair.

"I'm sure you are. You've done well." Nolan's smile faltered a bit after noticing a change in Bevin's face. "Are you all right?"

She took a deep breath and forced another smile. "Absolutely. I'm going to do a few errands. There's cheese and bread in the kitchen if you get hungry before dinner."

Adalyn watched as Bevin rose and left the group. She understood exactly how it felt to know that your life was about to change, and the worry about those you were leaving behind.

CHAPTER THREE

News of Bevin leaving the village spread quickly, and the group left a large gathering of weepy women and children behind as they departed. Bella handed them an extra pack of food that she had stayed up all night baking, and extended a small pouch of what Adalyn assumed was probably the extent of the gold the family currently had to her daughter as they loaded up to leave. The latter was safely tucked away out of sight before anyone else could see what was given.

Finally on their way, the party's mood perked up, and the walk through the well-worn forest roads was easy. As lunch time approached, a small town appeared over a ridge.

"We will stay there tonight," Bevin informed the group.

Nolan tossed a pebble and watched as it bounced off the trunk of an ancient tree. "Why are we stopping so soon? We still have most of the day ahead of us that we could travel."

"It's either sleep in a bed here and have a hot meal at the inn, or we sleep under the stars tonight. Either way, we will arrive at Trist tomorrow."

"We're really that close?" Adalyn asked.

"We are. We just can't get there by night fall. I know I would much rather sleep in the inn."

Adalyn turned to Venlian to gauge his opinion of the plan. His face was as hard to read as ever.

"Any thoughts?"

"She's not wrong; we can't get to Trist today," he answered. "Over the last five centuries, the exact distances in Chors has faded a bit in my mind, and I never spent much time here anyway. I mostly stayed with the war council in the Pieriun capital. I defer to Bevin's judgement on this one."

Deciding that was enough for her, Adalyn started down the hill with a skip in her step, "All right, let's get going, then. This may be our last chance at freedom for a while."

Nolan tossed another pebble and watched it ricochet off one tree trunk into another. "Expecting trouble, are you?"

She winked. "Always. Have you met me?"

Bevin picked up a handful of pebbles and began throwing them as well. The walk into town became a contest seeing who could make the most ridiculous shots with their pebbles. Multiple tree trunks; off of a moss-covered rock and into a fallen, hollowed out log; across the surface of the creek they crossed. Venlian, Adalyn, and Vaeren gave suggestions for challenges, but never participated themselves. By the time they reached the town, the entire group was cheering for the completed challenges and laughing at the failed ones.

Not much bigger than Bevin's village, the town of Shreem was quaint. It was really only upgraded to a town due to the small market around the town center, an inn, and the businesses of a blacksmith and clothmaker.

Bevin led the group towards the two-story wooden inn. The only improvement that the simple structure had over most of the others in the town were glass windows and an impressive set of horse stalls attached to the side of the building.

Once inside, the whitewashed walls and sunlight let in through the wavy glass gave the space a cheery air. Small flecks of dust glinted in the light of the almost empty dining area.

"Can we have two rooms for tonight?" Bevin asked the man behind the bar.

Adalyn wandered off as Bevin settled their lodgings for the night. The smell of fresh baked bread heavy in the air led her towards a basket at the end of the bar.

"How much for one of these?" Adalyn asked as she pointed at the linen-lined basket.

Handing a pair of keys to Bevin, the man walked over to her. "These are already claimed by the schoolchildren, but the next ones should be out of the oven soon. If you're hungry, I can bring some out to you. Is just cheese with it all right? My stew won't be ready for several more hours."

Nolan spoke up from behind Adalyn, making her jump. "That sounds great. We'll just take a seat over there. Thank you."

Adalyn joined the rest of the group at a wooden table

near one of the windows. A discussion was already underway by the time she sat down.

"I swear, it's true!" Bevin insisted with her hand over her heart.

Adalyn sat down between Nolan and Venlian. "What's true?"

Venlian shook his head. "I didn't say it wasn't true. I said that I wonder how many of the details were embellished. No one really knows what happened to the kingdom of Almendra. Even my books don't tell me what really happened. It's limited to the knowledge of those whose book it is."

Nolan, Vaeren, and Bevin gave him blank stares. Adalyn cracked a smile, knowing that she was probably the only one in the room who had any clue what Venlian was talking about. His library, filled with books that held the story of each person's life, had completely changed her world. Not only did she learn of her ability there, but it had also been where she'd seen the lives of Banneret who had come before her—several at a forge that she desperately wanted to find.

"Are you going to believe some dusty old books, or someone who lived near it as everything happened?"

Adalyn's curiosity was officially piqued. "As what happened?"

Bevin leaned both elbows on the table. "Only a few years ago, Almendra was a flourishing and thriving kingdom. We traded with them regularly and were on friendly terms. Something happened, though, and it all stopped."

"What do you mean, something happened?" Nolan also leaned forward on the table, his gaze locked on Bevin.

"All communication with them stopped. Chors sent people in to find out what happened, and no one ever returned."

An uneasy feeling twisted Adalyn's stomach. "Never?"

Bevin shook her head. "Never. Then things got even weirder. Creatures we had never seen before started to cross their borders and enter Chors. These weren't regular animals, either. The creatures that showed up were dark and twisted."

"Like death slaughs?" Adalyn asked, turning to Nolan.

Nolan's head snapped in her direction and their eyes locked.

"So you've seen them?"

Adalyn nodded. "A couple. They are almost impossible to kill."

"I assume you ultimately succeeded, though. You're still here, aren't you? There're many more dark creatures that come from Almendra than just death slaughs, though. We don't know where exactly they come from, just that no normal weapons can harm them. I assume this means they've entered Pieriun through the gates."

Nolan turned back to Bevin. "According to my people, they came through the gates during the war. We spent generations hunting them all down and killing them. The one that we dealt with was the first seen in hundreds of years."

"You're very blessed, then." Bevin looked at Venlian. "It's still hard to believe that so much time has passed."

"I admit it's sort of surreal to be back here and for nothing to have changed. I feel like I've stepped back into my past," Venlian responded.

"So you've been here before?"

"Only a handful of times. I have…" he paused, "*connections* in Chors. Ones that were left behind and sealed here with the spell."

A loud thunk made the group jump as a large platter of breads and cheeses was plopped in the center of the table. "Would anyone care for an ale or water?"

Adalyn still watched the haunted look on Venlian's face. "Can we get both for all of us, please?"

"Of course. I will grab that and be right back."

Adalyn couldn't help but wonder just what, or who, Venlian had left trapped here.

FAIR WEATHER MADE FOR A QUICK JOURNEY, AND even though they'd not hurried themselves, by evening they were entering the city gates of Trist.

"What do we do now?" Adalyn asked Venlian while eyeing the crowded streets they walked.

"Now we find somewhere to hole up and wait. I'm sure someone is already on their way to notify the king that we are here."

Her hand moved to her stomach as it growled from the smells of smoked meats and sweet fruits. "Why do you say that?"

Venlian nodded towards the edges of the street. "There are more soldiers following us the further into Trist we go. My face is known to them, and they don't know if I'm a threat or not."

As she looked closer at the crowd around them,

Adalyn spotted guards in the shadows and standing behind stalls, watching them, hands on their hilts and ready to move into action at a moment's notice.

"There's an inn further up the street. We can check if they have any empty rooms. They've got wonderful mead and apple tarts," Bevin offered.

"Lead the way," Venlian said, gesturing along the cobblestones.

The inn was better than Adalyn expected, a tall wooden building with sturdy furniture and not a speck of dust or crumb in sight, the owner and serving maids all just as put-together and tidy as the inn itself. It was a stark contrast to some of the buildings they had passed on their way through the capital.

The market they'd entered had soon transitioned to brothels. Brightly dressed women mingled in the street offering to entertain anyone who was in need of company. Beggars ducked into alleys as the women chased them away from their potential clients, only to reappear in the crowd soon after.

No, the inn they had found was much better than anywhere else they had encountered so far in Trist.

Venlian spoke to the owner to secure them rooms while the rest of the group claimed a table. A bard played music, and bowls of stew, a plate of apple tarts, and pints of mead appeared on their table soon after Venlian joined them.

"We have two rooms, men in one and women in the other. I don't imagine we will be here for more than a night," Venlian shared before biting into the flaky crust of a tart.

Nolan finished a long swig of his mead and slammed his empty pewter mug on the table. "Why exactly do you think that?"

Venlian's brow rose as he took note of Nolan's third mead being delivered. "Don't get too drunk. We don't know when the king will ask to see us, and most of the people in here will currently view us as enemies. Technically, they are still at war with us."

A sad look of longing crossed Nolan's face as he eyed another mug, but he chose to start on his stew instead.

"It's true. I heard a rumor that you were here, but I didn't dare believe it."

Venlian's head whipped around at the feminine voice.

"Sariah?" he asked, a warm smile lighting up his face.

Adalyn wasn't sure she had ever seen someone so beautiful. The candlelight reflected not only off of delicate armor, but off golden curls that framed the pointed ears and green eyes of the newcomer, making her seem even more magical.

Venlian rose and the two embraced. "What are you doing here?" he asked.

Her hands stayed on his arms as the two parted. "I'm here to ask you the same thing. What are you doing in Chors? Last I heard, you'd abandoned Pieriun's king and gone back to your books."

"I did, but things have changed. We are here to talk to King Garren about a truce. Dragmire and his daughter are both gone, and the current king of Pieriun doesn't wish to continue this war."

Adalyn's stomach twisted a bit watching the two of them. She had never seen Venlian act like this with anyone. Lost in her thoughts, she didn't notice Venlian trying to get her attention.

"Adalyn, are you all right?"

"Yeah, sorry. I think I just need some rest," she answered, squirming under his gaze.

He drew a key from his pocket and reached across the table. "I understand. Second floor, third door on the right. Tomorrow morning we go to see the king."

Taking the key from him, Adalyn rose. "I'll be ready."

As she turned to leave, Nolan rose and touched her shoulder. "Let me come with you. I should sleep some of this off, anyways."

She nodded, and after Venlian gave Nolan his key, the two waved goodbye and headed up the stairs to their rooms.

Fumbling with the key at her door, Adalyn turned to bid Nolan goodnight only to find him directly in front of her. Her breath caught at being caught in his gaze.

He brushed a hair from her face before he leaned down and gently kissed her lips. Pulling back, his eyes searched her face for her reaction.

She lifted her hand to brush his cheek. "Sleep well, Nolan. I'll see you in the morning."

Adalyn turned, unlocked the door, and entered her room. Nolan still stood in the hall as she gently closed the door. She leaned her forehead on the door as she listened to him walk to the room next door and enter, her heart aflutter and her mind thoroughly confused.

A FULL ESCORT ARRIVED AT THE INN TO BRING THEM to the king. Having worked in King Coeus's kitchen and slept in the castle, Adalyn thought she wouldn't be as affected by the castle in Chors, but as they got closer and the actual size of it became apparent, she felt herself shrink a tiny bit more with each step.

Unlike the capital in Pieriun, which was sprawled over a mountain with all of the buildings covered in dark blue roofs, Trist was mostly greys and browns. The city showed the wear and tear that war had wreaked on it. The only able men visible wore uniforms, and the women and children all looked slightly worn. Thin fabric draped on the slightly too thin bodies of both soldiers and citizens.

The stark contrast between her kingdom, which had had time to recover from the war, and this one only strengthened Adalyn's determination to bring peace to Chors. Pieriun wanted no part in the war, and it broke her heart to picture her kingdom in a similar state to this one.

Armed men lined the top of the grey stone castle walls. She could feel their eyes following her party as they entered the castle grounds. Metal clashing and shouts from around the large courtyard only made her feel the effects of a kingdom at war more real, even if it was just training bouts.

Nolan strode in with his shoulders back and a very serious expression that said he meant business. Bevin was beside him, her eyes alight as she viewed what she hoped would be her near future. Vaeren's shoulders were hunched as he tentatively moved forward, wringing his hands. Venlian almost looked worried, as well, which concerned Adalyn a bit. She had never seen him look unsure about anything, and he was the only one of them who had an idea of what they were walking into beyond those giant wooden doors.

The tightness in her chest became worse with each step as they got closer to the throne room. Stopped in front of the last door while waiting to be allowed entry, Adalyn shared what she hoped was an encouraging smile with each of her group for those few seconds that seemed to last forever. Light peeked through the crack of the doors as it opened, and the group stepped through as they were announced.

Soldiers stood at attention next to each pillar that lined the edges of the room, and a small gathering of well-dressed individuals stood at the other end. Several men in fine clothes stood behind King Garren's massive, carved throne, including an elf who looked strikingly similar to the one who walked beside her.

King Garren watched the group approach him, his intense gaze looking through bushy brows down his straight nose. His bright red clothes seemed bold in the rather dreary-looking room.

Adalyn stopped in front of the throne and watched Venlian to see what he would do. Should she bow or speak? The realization that she should have asked what to do at this point *before* they left the inn only made the tightness over her heart firmer.

A moment of silence passed before Venlian bowed his head. "King Garren, thank you for being willing to see us."

"What brings a party from our enemy to my home?"

The deep rumble of the king's voice sent chills down Adalyn's spine.

"We've been sent by the king of Pieriun to discuss a truce with your kingdom."

"Your king knows I'm not interested in a truce unless he comes to submit himself."

Venlian pulled a letter from a pocket and held it out towards the king. "Things have changed in Pieriun. There is a new king who does not want to fight. He wants for both kingdoms to prosper."

A snort came from one of the nobles behind the king.

Adalyn shot him a look. She was quickly becoming frustrated with their cold reception.

"I promise that it's true, your majesty," Adalyn said, daring to look the king in the eyes. "We wouldn't have made the journey through your lands if it wasn't."

"Just who do you think you are, to speak to me so boldly?"

"Adalyn Mernt, commander of the Banneret and here as a representative of my king. King Coeus wants to put this war to an end and give our kingdoms a chance to be friendly."

"Who in the nine realms is Coeus? You think you can fool me? We've been at war for years. Glenda is the commander of the Banneret, not you," King Garren spat at her.

Venlian indicated the letter again. "It's all been explained in this."

A soldier took it from Venlian and carried it to the king, who only eyed it before looking back at their party.

"How do I know that this doesn't have a trap? A spell or poison?"

Adalyn threw out her arm and offered her gloveless hand. "For goodness' sake, give it to me. I will open it for you! If it is safe, will you just read it?"

Wrath practically rolled off the king in waves.

Adalyn stared him down. One part of her brain was telling her that she needed to shut up and run, and another that she was here with the authority of her king. She couldn't come across as weak.

A small nod of the king's head, and the letter was placed in her hand. She cracked the seal, and it took every ounce of restraint she had to stop herself from dramatically waving the paper in front of her and licking it to prove that there was nothing wrong with the letter. Only the knowledge that she was here as a high-level representative, and the image of King Coeus's face should he find out about such antics, stopped her. Instead, she held it out with force and waited for someone to take it from her.

The letter finally made it into the king's hands, and the entire room waited for him to read it. His expression shifted from anger to confusion as he turned from one page to the next.

"How… how can this be true?"

Adalyn's frustration eased a bit at the change in his demeanor. At least he wasn't completely dismissing the information before him. "I swear it all is. We have already sent out the order to recall troops from your land."

"Zephyr, is what they are saying true?"

The elf she'd noticed earlier stepped forward and

studied them. His eyes locked onto Venlian and stayed there as he answered. “I see no sign of them deceiving us.”

The king nodded. “I still need to verify what you are saying myself. I don’t want my kingdom to be at war, but this is still too far-fetched for me to believe on blind faith. You will stay in guest quarters in my castle while I investigate this. Do not attempt to leave.”

The humans in their party all nodded. Venlian only stared back at the elf studying him.

“I know who Venlian is, and you’ve told me who you are. I’m unfamiliar with the markings of one of your party, and am unsure why you are traveling with someone from my own kingdom.” The king pointed at each person as he spoke.

Nolan stepped forward and bowed. “I’m Nolan, a representative from the queen of Dunshire. I come in good faith and with the authority to discuss matters to help our kingdoms begin a relationship in peace.” He pulled out a letter of his own. “Would you like for me to open this one, as well?”

The king nodded, and Nolan cracked the seal on the parchment, unfolded the letter, and handed it to a soldier.

“Once I have verified their story, we will meet to discuss what will happen between our two kingdoms.”

Nolan smiled and stepped back next to Bevin. “Of course. Thank you.”

“And you? Why is one of my own people here with these outsiders?”

Bevin stepped forward. “I’m Bevin Thornglove from the village of Trush. I’ve been part of the watch at the gate near us. I've had several interactions with these people, and have seen Pieriun soldiers leaving through the gate."

"You've personally seen this?"

"I have."

"Why have you come here?"

She fidgeted under his intense gaze. "I wish to join your guard."

"You came here to request to join my guard, as a woman, even though you also knew that if I believed your company about this," the king waved the letters in the air, "the war would end and I would have no need to lower myself to bringing women among my ranks?"

"Yes, your majesty. That's correct." Bevin straightened and stood tall, with only a slight tremor giving her nerves away.

The king was silent for a moment as he contemplated what to do. "I have hope that this checks out. I don't want to be at war any longer. My people are suffering for it. You," he pointed at Bevin, "report to the guard house and ask for Terrence. Gerald will escort you. I am not admitting you to the guard yet, but I will allow for you to train with them while I verify this, as a thank you for assisting in potentially bringing our people peace."

Adalyn couldn't help but wonder if he was really doing it as a reward for her, or if he was truly doing it to keep a close eye on her. It turned her stomach to know that if something went wrong, her newfound friend would be punished for it as well.

"As for you," the king said, indicating the rest of their group, "I will have you stay in the castle's guest wing.

While you are not prisoners, as I investigate this I do request that you do not leave the castle grounds."

Still looking at Zephyr, Venlian responded, "Understood. We will stay in your guest wing and remain on the grounds."

"I have other business to attend to. Zephyr will show you where you will be situated. Please let him know if you need anything."

Dismissed, the group quickly left the hall and followed Zephyr down a long path of twisting stone hallways. Bevin had been taken to guard house, and the other four walked through the halls in silence. Each of them cast telling glances at each other, wondering who would speak first. Vaeren shook his head quickly, and Venlian was impassive.

Nolan was the one to break the silence. "Can I ask you a question, Zephyr?"

"Of course. I don't promise that I will give you an answer you want, but I promise that I will give you an answer."

"Fair enough. How could you tell we weren't lying?"

Zephyr glanced at Venlian again as they turned around a corner and started to ascend a spiral staircase. "It's an ability I have been blessed with as an elf."

"So, can all elves do this?"

"No; every elf has their own ability. Much like your Banneret each have their own gifts, elves do as well."

Adalyn thought about that. She hadn't spent much time with any Banneret other than her spirit friends who waited for her back in the Capital, and none of them could use their abilities in their current form. They hadn't discussed that they all had different ways in which they could use their magic.

"Is it your only ability?" Adalyn asked, her curiosity piqued.

"No, I have several."

They stayed silent, hoping he would elaborate, but he never did. Venlian continued to watch his fellow elf as they exited the staircase and began walking down another set of halls.

"Your ability is the only way you knew we were telling the truth?" he asked.

Zephyr's steady pace faltered for a moment as he glanced quickly at him. "It was."

"You don't think the word of your own son would have been enough?"

Adalyn choked on her own spit and coughed. Vaeren slapped her back a couple times, which was less helpful than intended.

Zephyr stopped, but didn't turn around. "My son has never lied to me in the past, but it's clear to me that you are not the same son that I last saw. You chose the wrong side."

Venlian's face twisted as his emotions began breaking through the mask he'd put over them. "I chose the side that I thought I could convince to stop the fighting, the pointless slaughter that was caused by human fervor."

Zephyr slowly turned around and faced Venlian. "Yes. How did that go?"

"Not as planned."

"What exactly do you mean, not as planned?"

Venlian finally looked away. "They ended the war, but not with a method I found acceptable."

"Venlian, what aren't you telling me?" Zephyr asked, saying his son's name for the first time. "Why don't you look like the son I last saw?"

Still avoiding Zephyr's gaze, Venlian spoke barely above a whisper, "They cast a spell that trapped this entire continent in time for five hundred years." He turned to face their guide. "At this point, Father, I'm older than you are."

CHAPTER FOUR

"What did you just say?" Zephyr's face paled.

Venlian stepped towards the elf. "I said I'm older than you are, Father. You've been trapped here, inside the spell, and are six-hundred and fifty-three years old. I'm eight-hundred eighty-nine."

Zephyr backed away with horror in his eyes. "No! They couldn't have."

Everyone in the group stood in silence and watched as he processed the news.

"Your mother?"

"She is back home. Waiting for you."

"I just… this can't be real."

Venlian stepped towards his father and extended his arm. "You're welcome to check."

Zephyr grabbed his hand and closed his eyes. Taking a deep breath, he opened them and looked into Venlian's eyes. What little color he still had drained from his face.

His body shook as he pulled away again. "I need… time."

Adalyn looked Venlian over. Not only had the fact that Zephyr was Venlian's father shocked her, but how was it possible that he could be that old? She knew that elves lived longer than humans, but it didn't seem possible that the combined age of their party was close to a millennium. Sure, Venlian was more serious and seemed wise, but she had chalked that up to him just being an elf—not that she had met many other elves. She'd known that Venlian had been part of the war five hundred years ago, but it hadn't really dawned on her just how old her friend truly was. It made her wonder what else she didn't know.

Zephyr turned back around and started down the hall again.

Nolan quickly followed, Vaeren trailing after him. Adalyn stood still for a moment, watching Venlian. He watched his father walk away for a moment before again wiping the emotion from his face and moving forward. Adalyn did the same.

Several turns later, Zephyr opened a set of doors into a large suite.

"This is one of the family suites. While I know you are not technically family to one another, I thought it would be best to give you a space where you could be together outside of the prying eyes of the court. Some of them mean well; some of them really don't, though."

The group stepped into the large sitting room, and as Adalyn turned around to thank Zephyr for escorting them there, he cleared his throat. "If you need anything, you only need to ask a guard outside. If you leave this room, you will need an escort. And Venlian—I'm glad that you're safe, my son."

He stepped through the door and quickly closed it behind him.

Venlian silently opened one of the other five doors and walked through, closing it behind him.

"I guess he's picked that room. Want to take a peek and decide which one you want?" Nolan offered.

"You and Vaeren can decide first. I want to explore a bit."

He shot her a wicked grin. "You and your adventures." He walked over to a door and opened it. "Nope, not taking this one unless none of you use the bathroom. This tub is big enough that I could sleep in it."

Adalyn rushed over to take a look. She couldn't believe her eyes. She would have thought that in the five hundred years since the war ended the first time that Pieriun would have advanced in their bathroom usage, but apparently the rich in Chors were well taken care of. A massive copper tub sat in the middle of the room with a carved wooden chest of drawers nearby. A floral painted wash basin and pitcher sat on top, and a large gold mirror hung above. A bench was built along the outside wall. Walking over to investigate, Adalyn lifted a wooden lid to find a hole in the bench dropping into empty air outside.

"I wonder what this is?" Adalyn wondered to herself.

Nolan's voice made her jump. She had forgotten that he was in here with her. "A toilet. I've seen them in a few castles that we stop at. It drops below, and servants clear it away every few days to prevent the castle grounds from piling up."

"You're kidding me."

He crossed his arms and he shook his head, a goofy

grin filling his face. "Nope, I'm completely serious. You keep exploring, I'm going to go pick my room."

Left alone for the first time in days, Adalyn took a deep breath and nearly gagged. While the servants may carry away the pile below, the smell was still potent. Replacing the lid over the hole and checking that it was secure, she exited the bathroom and left to investigate the sitting room.

A large fireplace with several large chairs and ottomans on fur rugs in front of it lined one wall between two of the bedrooms. The other half of the room was dominated by a table and chairs, and the wall between the bathroom and the room Venlian had chosen was lined with book shelves and a desk. The outside wall had several large windows that let sunlight in, and a door opened up to a balcony outside.

Only one door was still open, and Adalyn assumed it must be her bedroom. Entering the space, she took in the small dresser and matching side table. Apparently the set included the massive four post bed that took up most of the space.

She walked over and plopped herself onto the pile of pillows at the head of the bed. At that moment, she decided that being a temporary prisoner might not be so bad after all.

Adalyn didn't even remember falling asleep. The last thing she remembered was laying down on the bed, and the next thing she knew, she was waking up with everything pitch black. It took her a few minutes to find a candle, but she had no way to light it. Venturing out of her room, she realized a servant must have come into their suite while she was asleep and lit the fireplace in the main room. Taking her candle over to the fire, she used the flames from the fireplace to light it. Her hand burned from the intense heat radiating out.

Her stomach rumbled, reminding her that she hadn't eaten anything yet today. She had been too nervous to eat at the inn before they came to see the king.

Peeking her head out the suite door, she saw no guards. Odd, considering they'd been informed that they would be watched and not allowed to leave their suite unattended.

She closed the door quietly behind her and slowly walked down the hall. She wasn't sure where the kitchens were, but she hoped that if she looked long enough she would find some source of food somewhere.

The flicker of her lonely candle cast shadows on the walls as she worked her way down. Her best guess was that she would find the kitchen on the bottom level, but no set of stairs seemed to go from the top to the bottom of the castle in one go. Smart way to protect themselves in an invasion, but terrible for trying to find your way around.

After spending so much time wandering that she was hopelessly lost, a hint of spices hit her nose and made her stomach rumble. She chose to follow the smell in hopes that she would soon find something very yummy.

Soon a doorway opened into a kitchen even larger than the one she had worked in in Pieriun. Movement from the corner made her freeze, and she jumped a moment later when a voice came from a different direction.

"Don't mind her," the feminine voice said softly.

Adalyn whipped around, almost dropping her candle. "I'm so sorry, I didn't realize that there was anyone in here."

"No worries." A tall blonde woman with a sharp nose moved into the glow from the massive fireplace. "That's just one of the kitchen maids. She sleeps in here to keep the fire going through the night."

Looking back at where she had first seen movement, Adalyn noticed a tuft of curly hair sticking out from the top of a lump of blankets.

"Can I help you with anything? You don't look familiar. Are you lost?"

"Just very hungry."

A warm smile crossed the lady's face. "A woman after my own heart. There's some leftover cake under the cabinet over there and a bucket of water by the door. I'm afraid most of our produce has recently been preserved, so we don't have much in the way of fresh food to offer at the moment."

"Thank you."

Adalyn walked over to the cabinet and peeked under the cloth covering a mouth-watering chunk of chocolate cake. Lifting the plate out of the cabinet, she also grabbed a small fork and a cup from the counter above and proceeded to dip it for a fresh cup of water. Rejoining her unexpected dinner companion, she settled on a stool at one of the work tables.

"I'm Neith," the blonde woman offered, looking at Adalyn expectantly.

"Adalyn."

"Ah… That's why I don't know your face. You're with the party from Pieriun."

Adalyn nearly choked on her first glorious bite. What had initially been delicious and moist suddenly felt dry in her mouth.

"That would be me. How did you know?"

"Word travels fast among the royal court. You really came here for a truce?"

"We did. There's no one left in Pieriun who was part of the original war. We have no issue with Chors and only want to develop a good relationship."

Neith watched Adalyn as she took another bite. "I'm surprised they let you out of your guest suite unattended." Picking up a fork from her own empty plate, she took a bite of the cake herself and released a small sigh. "I swear I'm always hungry. It's very rare for me to ever feel truly full."

Adalyn wondered if maybe this was a cake that the moisture sapped right out of as soon as it hit your mouth, because so far every bite had done this.

"I wasn't exactly given permission. I opened the door to ask for food and there were no guards outside."

"None at all?"

Adalyn shook her head and washed down the last bite with surprisingly sweet tasting water.

"I will mention it…" Neith began, but paused when Adalyn's hand shot out to touch her arm, "without mentioning that you were here. I promise. Just to make sure that you have a way to get what you need when you need it."

Adalyn pulled her hand back. "Thank you. Sorry, I didn't mean to jump out like that."

"No need to apologize. I understand your concern. I'm sure we will be seeing much more of each other, Adalyn. It was good to meet you in person."

"You, too."

Watching Neith leave, Adalyn took another bite of cake and let it sit in her mouth for a moment, this time enjoying the way it melted in her mouth. At least this part of the cake didn't appear to be faulty.

HER TRAVELING MUST HAVE WORN HER OUT MORE than she'd realized, and the sun was high in the sky by the time she woke up. Entering the sitting room, she found Nolan picking from a large platter of food while Vaeren read by the fire.

"Good afternoon, sleepyhead."

"What? Afternoon? There's no way I slept that long!"

His wicked grin assured her that it wasn't possible he was wrong about this.

"It's really afternoon?"

"Yep. You aren't the only one who slept in. Venlian hasn't been out yet, either."

Adalyn glanced over at his door. "Really? That's odd. Do elves really even sleep? I've always sort of pictured them basically just meditating while at rest."

Nolan shrugged. "I honestly have no clue. He does lay

down to rest, but I don't think I've ever seen him actually go into a deep sleep."

She raised a brow. "You've been watching him sleep?"

"You know it's not like that. Technically, you've seen it, too, when we slept outside."

She shook her head. "I always saw him leaning on a tree and still alert. I've never even seen him lay down."

"Maybe he just hasn't been able to relax around us enough to sleep."

The thought hadn't ever crossed her mind. She thought that they had become friends, but what if he found them to be more of a responsibility than real friends? What if he couldn't be himself around her? There were moments when Venlian seemed relaxed with her, but Adalyn realized she had never seen him act that way when they were with anyone else.

"Anyways, I'm going to go for a walk with our friendly escorts out there. I want to check in and see how Bevin is holding up. Want to come?"

Her chest tightened, and Adalyn felt confused for a moment. "Another time? I'm starving. All I've had since we got here was chocolate cake."

"Wait, there's cake?"

Realizing what she had just said, she gave only the smallest explanation. "I woke up hungry late last night and got some. Sorry, I didn't get any to share."

Nolan stood and planted a light kiss on her cheek. "Don't worry, I forgive you. I'll be back soon. I just don't like being cooped up for too long and not knowing my surroundings."

"I completely understand. Stay out of trouble."

"Well, you're no fun," Nolan said with a wave as he left the suite.

Adalyn grabbed a slice of fruit bread and wandered over to a bookshelf to investigate what it had to offer. Her finger brushed across the leather bindings, all unfamiliar books, in a mix of what she assumed were stories and historical records. She was dying to know if *A Water Dragon and His Mate: The Origin of Mermaids* was a book of fact or fiction. Just as she pulled it off the shelf, a knock sounded at the door.

Book in hand, she walked over and opened it. "How may I help you?"

A small group of soldiers dressed in black filled the hall outside their room.

"Your party has been summoned by the king."

"Oh, I see. There's only two of us ready here at the moment…"

"I'm ready, we can leave as soon as you are." Venlian looked as perfect as ever as he appeared next to her. She'd assumed that his lack of appearance had been due to him sleeping or dealing with his father from the day before, but nothing seemed amiss.

Placing the book on a table near the door, she tossed her hair in a bun as Vaeren crossed the room to join the crowd near the door.

"I'm ready, let's go."

The soldiers surrounded them as they walked through the maze of hallways and stairs back towards the throne room. Adalyn accepted that even if she wanted or needed to escape, she would never find her way out of this castle without jumping to her death.

Without stopping, the group entered the throne room and made their way up to the king. Adalyn glanced behind the king as she rose from a small bow and noted that Zephyr was there among several other members of the court.

"I've heard back from some of my scouts," the king began without preamble. "It currently appears that you are, in fact, telling the truth about the Pieriun army retreating. Between these reports and Zephyr's ability, I choose to believe your claims to want an end to the war."

"That's wonderful news!" Adalyn responded, practically bouncing on the balls of her feet. This was going better than she'd expected.

"I have read through the letters from King Coeus and Queen Tillie," King Garren continued. "I have questions about some discrepancies."

With a tilt of his head, Venlian shifted his eyes between his father and the king. "Oh? What sort of questions?"

"The letter…"

A loud knock on the door echoed through the room.

King Garren looked displeased, but waved his hand to indicate that the doors should be opened, revealing the last people Adalyn expected to see. The figures seemed too large for the grand hall they now entered, all of them having to duck as they crossed the threshold.

Four golems thudded up next to Adalyn and Venlian and bowed.

"King Garren, it's good to see you again." The white shine off of Merit's stone body almost glowed in the dour room.

"Merit! It's been far too long. What brings you here?" King Garren's face lit up with the entrance of what appeared to be his old friend.

The golems rose from their bows.

"That it has," Merit responded. "I'm here not only for a chance to see an old friend, but also to relay a message."

King Garren leaned forward on this throne. "Proceed."

"I'm here as a representative of the dwarven king, Thanmog, to help with discussions of this delicate time."

"I'm unaware of a King Thanmog. What mountain does he reside in?"

"The one under the capital of Pieriun."

Zephyr spoke up from the left side of the king. "There is no dwarven king under the capital."

"Shows just how much you know," Carnelian, the red golem, muttered.

Clunks ricocheted through the hall as both Iolite and Lazuli smacked him to shut him up.

Merit cleared his throat. "Please excuse my friend. After your kingdom was trapped in a spell, the king hunted down anyone who wasn't human. Elves retreated to their land, and the dwarves, unable to return here through the gates, sacrificed part of their people to go into hiding under the mountain below the capital."

"He always was a crazy old coot."

Adalyn eyed the young man on the king's right hand who had spoken.

King Garren shot him dirty look. "You played your part in driving the king and his daughter mad, my son. If it weren't for you and your whims, we wouldn't be in this mess to begin with."

While Adalyn felt her jaw drop, she noticed that no one else in the room seemed surprised by this statement. She'd heard part of what had happened, but hearing it confirmed by King Garren and seeing the prince herself wasn't what she'd expected.

The king redirected his attention back to Merit. "You've been part of what's happened in Pieriun?"

"I have."

King Garren redirected his attention back to Adalyn, Venlian, and Vaeren. "I wish to speak more with the representative of the dwarf king before we continue this discussion. You are excused."

No one had to tell Adalyn to leave twice. Being in the king's presence made her feel guilty without having done anything wrong. She did wonder, though, just what discrepancy he had found in the letters.

CHAPTER FIVE

Adalyn desperately wanted to talk to the golems and find out why they were really in Chors. She knew that they didn't consider themselves to be under King Thanmog's rule, which meant that more than likely they were there for her.

With Venlian back in his room and Nolan still gone, she settled down near Vaeren by the fireplace with the book she had discovered, *A Water Dragon and His Mate: The Origin of Mermaids*. The story of a water dragon falling in love with a fisherman's daughter reeled her in as the relationship turned from fear and misunderstandings to a much softer love. She could almost see it in her mind as they fought their families to be together and eventually ran away to live in a cave away from everyone they knew.

An idea struck her after turning a page. What if she could look into this book like she had the ones in Venlian's library? She had always assumed that she could do it with his because they were magical and unique, but what if it was in fact her own ability that had made it possible?

Adalyn took the book to her room for privacy and sat on the bed. Taking a deep breath, she felt the pages between her fingers and pictured the cave as she had imagined it in her mind. She felt a sudden pull on her ability, and soon found herself standing in a slightly different, but very similar, cave—a vast cavern where the blue of the water reflected off of the ceiling as small fins the color of her blade disturbed the otherwise still pool that took over a majority of the space.

Entranced by the movement of fins in the water, she almost missed that the other half of these fish were not fish at all, but actually infants. No longer than her fingertip to her elbow, the group of tiny mermaids bumped into each other in the enclosed pool.

A small cry sounded as one of their head's breached the surface, only to submerge back under immediately.

Adalyn quickly moved away from the edge of the pool and hid behind a large rock at the sound of footsteps hurrying her way. She knew that in Venlian's books no one could see her, but she wasn't sure if that's how it would work in a book that wasn't an actual record of someone's life.

The dirtied hem of a damp skirt shuffled past her and the sound of a body entering the water peeked her curiosity. A brunette human woman sat in the pool and pulled two of the small mermaids to her breasts and fed them as they stayed submerged.

Adalyn didn't know just what to think. Truly, she had never really imagined that mermaids could exist, let alone how they started out or what they ate. If she had, this definitely wouldn't have been it.

"Our little ones are hungry, are they?" a husky voice said as a tall man with a slight blue hue to his skin and the brightest eyes she had ever seen walked over to the woman in the pool.

The woman responded, her voice almost musical as she laughed. "When are they not?"

The man climbed into the pool with her and shifted into a large dragon. His brood of tiny mermaids who weren't feeding swarmed towards him and cuddled up next to him.

"You love your father, don't you? Who knew that the big, bad Torrent would be such a big softy?"

A rumble of bubbles came to the surface as a response from the dragon.

Adalyn stayed for a few moments and watched the happy family. Even if this was only a fairytale, she wished she had more memories of these types of moments with her own family. Her heart began to ache, and she released her ability to allow herself to return to her room in Chors.

Closing the book and setting it on her nightstand, she decided that it was time for a walk. She had no clue how long she had been sitting while she was inside the book, but her body ached as if it had been an entire day.

Opening the suite door, she found a pair of guards and asked them to take her to the training grounds. Vaeren had told her that Nolan had yet to return, and she was curious how Bevin was fairing.

Their guest suite was closer to the grounds than she expected. It only took one flight of stairs and a few seemingly unnecessary turns to make it outside.

The glint of steel in the sun as it clashed against others

with so many people in the courtyard almost blinded her as she looked for her friends. Spotting them near the wall not too far away, she began to walk towards them and suddenly stopped.

The two crossed swords, pushing each other back, neither wanting to give the other any ground. Nolan pushed up with a shield and knocked Bevin off balance, who landed on her back. Reaching out, Nolan helped her back up.

Adalyn watched the interaction. Her stomach twisted into knots as Nolan reached up and wiped a tear from Bevin's face. Bevin quickly rose an arm and wiped her face on the back of her leathers. Red seeped along the bottom of her sleeve and trickled down her fingertips.

As Nolan reached for Bevin's hand, Adalyn quickly turned and returned to the guest suite. Processing what she had just seen, she told herself that he was only training Bevin. Helping her, really, and even if he wasn't… she and him weren't anything official, anyways.

She held her tears back just barely; she only wanted to retreat into her room, but was greeted by an entourage of golems in the sitting room instead.

She took a deep breath to steady her nerves. "I wasn't expecting to see you in our room."

While the guest suite was rather large, it seemed tiny with four large stone bodies inside it.

"How could we come all this way and not see you?" Lazuli replied.

"King Thanmog sent you, or so you said. Was he worried we wouldn't be able to do this?"

"Oh, he wasn't the one who asked us to come here.

He's quite happy in his home under your capital," Carnelian chipped in. A groan of distress emitted from the couch as he chuckled at the idea.

Adalyn gave them a questioning look. "Who sent you, then?"

Lazuli piped in from near a large art piece on the wall. "Your own king, my dear. He needs you."

"What could he need me for?"

Lazuli leaned in closer to the painting and touched it with the tip of her stone finger. "I love when I find art made of the same material as myself. It's almost as if it calls to me," she murmured before she turned to face Adalyn again. "*You* are who he entrusted the Banneret to. They've been coming back for more than two months now, and there have definitely been some problems."

"Eridu needs direction, and your king needs to discuss a few complications that have arisen," Iolite added.

A small piece off of the back of the couch fell to the floor as Carnelian rested his arm on it. "Complications—that's one way to put it. Basically, all hell has broken loose because of your soldiers, and you gotta fix it."

Adalyn's mind reeled at what they were saying. Her brain was struggling to wrap it's brain around what she had just witnessed between Nolan and Bevin, and now yet another item was added to her plate of things to stress over. On the other hand, this may be just the distraction that she needed while she processed everything. Questions could be asked later—once she had cooled down. Adalyn's emotional distress about her relationship was quickly turning to frustration.

"All right, I will figure out a way to head back. I'm not

sure if King Garren will let me out of here, or… wait a minute." Adalyn turned towards Merit. "Why exactly were you guys chosen to come here? There are literally hundreds of golems in Pieriun. How do you know King Garren?"

Merit's chin rose. "We're old friends. Before I became a golem, I was a prince of my mountain clan. I was even at Garren's wedding. Actually, I helped supply the stone for this addition that you are currently staying in."

Adalyn's temper was running short. "So why weren't you sent here instead of me to begin with?"

He shrugged. "They never asked."

She could almost feel steam coming off of her. "And you never thought to offer?"

Iolite stepped in. "Remember, we stay out of the politics of mortals as much as is possible. It's part of our agreement to become golems."

"Nope, not good enough. You," Adalyn pointed at Merit, "are going to come help me convince the king to let me head back to Pieriun for a bit."

"That's not necessary," Venlian's smooth voice cut instantly through her anger. Was that one of his elvish abilities? "You can worldwalk back. They never need to know that you were gone."

"I can do that from here? I thought the time difference would cause issues."

"It might, but I think you've advanced your skills far enough that you could make it work. You will feel a resistance as you go through what remains of the living spell, though."

The wheels in her brain began to turn as she thought about how exactly she could make this work. She would need somewhere safe to go and keep track of time to ensure that no one realized she was missing.

Nodding her head, she spoke to no one in particular, "All right, I can do it. You said it has been two months there, and it's been just over two days here. It's not exact, but if I consider a day there an hour here, I can do short trips without raising any alarms."

"I would suggest waiting until tonight," Venlian added. "Perhaps rest a bit first. It will give you more time to be over there without anyone expecting to see you here."

As much as she wanted to run away from the vision in her head, she knew he was right.

"That's smart, I can do that. By the way," Adalyn said, directing her attention back to the golems, "I'm sorry. I shouldn't have snapped. It's been a rough day. Tell me a bit about what's been going on in Pieriun while we've been away."

CHAPTER SIX

The immediate change from her plush bed in Chors to her usual firm straw mattress in Pieriun told Adalyn that she had, in fact, worldwalked back. The intense wave of exhaustion and need to empty everything from her stomach told her that Venlian was correct—getting through the living spell that was still on Chors was at the extent of what her ability could currently handle.

After filling the bowl in her chamber with the limited contents of her stomach, she let the darkness claim her as she recovered from the exertion.

"I thought I felt you join us," Glenda's voice roused Adalyn from a deep sleep, and the bright blue glow of her friend's body dimly lit the room.

Adalyn groaned. "You felt me?"

"You forget that we are connected through our shared ability. Normally, only one with this ability is alive at a time. While I can't use it, enough is still a part of me that it sometimes feels the pull towards itself in you."

The thought that things could be difficult after Glenda was freed from the spell crossed Adalyn's mind for a moment, but she quickly brushed it away. Remembering that she had a limited amount of time to be here sent a sense of urgency through her.

"How long have I been here?"

"A few hours. I let you rest before rousing you. The castle is starting to wake, and there's drama in your friend's office already."

Forever grateful that Eridu had accepted the request to help the Banneret, Adalyn could only imagine what her dwarven friend had put up with. She rolled out of bed and smoothed her hands over her hair, ignoring the knots and quickly throwing it into a low bun.

"All right, let's do this."

Adalyn could already hear the muffled shouts of several men coming from behind the wooden door of Eridu's office before she even turned the last corner in the hallway. Adrenaline pumped through her and she quickened her steps, quietly opened the door, and slipped in unnoticed.

"How could you possibly understand? You don't even have magic!" a tall man with blond hair bellowed while leaning on her friend's desk.

"I understand why this frustrates you, and we are doing the best that we can. I promise you, though, that while I am unable to use magic in the way that you do, I do understand it quite well and am capable of using it in my own way." Eridu sat in a large wooden chair with her hands folded in her lap, looking as if this was nothing to her.

A burly man ran his hand through his red scruffy beard and let out a frustrated sigh. "We're not saying that you aren't good at enchantments. We know that dwarves are well versed in that. What we are saying is that you are not a Banneret. There needs to be someone in charge of the Banneret who can understand everything about us. Someone who can solve the more unique problems that we deal with."

Glenda spoke from beside Adalyn. "Unique problems? The unique problems that they are dealing with are similar to what the dwarves dealt with, as well. She's much smarter than they give her credit for. If only they would listen."

Eridu's voice remained calm. "I've been placed in this position by the captain of the Banneret with the support of King Coeus. If you would discuss your unique problems with me, I could help resolve them."

The blond man spat as he spoke. "The captain of the Banneret? For all we know, she doesn't even exist."

Adalyn took that as her cue. "Oh, I exist."

The men spun around, wide-eyed, and Eridu's face transformed into a relieved smile. Their eyes darted to the captain pin on her blue wool uniform and down to the sword at her side.

Adalyn crossed her arms and leaned on the wall behind her. "Now, what is it that you need help with?"

Neither man spoke.

"They, along with many others, are having some trouble adjusting to the changes in Pieriun since they left," Eridu stated. "Reasonably so, in my opinion."

"Ah, I understand. Are there any specific things that

you men feel should be looked after first?"

Another moment of silence passed before one of the men snapped out of his stupor. "You are the captain of the Banneret?"

"Yes."

"Joe," Glenda told Adalyn helpfully.

"I am the captain of the Banneret, Joe."

Watching the shocked look reappear on his face brought more glee than Adalyn had thought possible.

The other man spoke. "How do you know who he is?"

"Triston," Glenda offered again.

"We're not alone in here, Triston. In fact, you've never been without a captain. Your old one has been here all along, only you couldn't see her."

"Idiot," Glenda muttered.

"I would like to add that she's not very pleased."

Glenda laughed. "That's an understatement!"

Adalyn smirked, fighting to restrain her laughter. "Do you have any new complaints that you wish to present to my second-in-command?"

Both men shook their heads.

"All right, you are both dismissed, then. I will discuss matters with Eridu and the king. I promise that we will try to do the best we can to make this work. I suggest, though, that you spread the word that I will not put up with this kind of behavior. I am on a mission for your king and will be gone for extended periods of time." Adalyn fixed them with a stern look and pointed to Eridu. "What she says, goes."

Heads nodding, the men left the room as quickly as they could get their bodies to move.

A slow clap from Eridu brought a smile to Adalyn's face. "Who knew that Adalyn Mernt could be so… commanding?"

"Certainly not me. Has it been this rough the entire time I've been gone?"

"Not the entire time, but it's definitely getting worse as more people show up."

Adalyn moved to sit in the chair across from Eridu. "Are there commanders coming back as well as soldiers? What about Brinn? He seemed reasonable."

"He's one of your biggest supporters and has been a big help. The problem is that he's the only one here who has seen you. There're so many men coming home to their families gone, homes having rotted away, and no direction to focus their distress and anger. I don't really know what to do. Their ranks are still in order, but the leaders are still in Chors or had been wiped out by the old king. There's a big gap, and I don't have the authority to adjust that."

Adalyn thought for a moment.

"I will talk with the king and see what he has planned. These problems aren't just within the Banneret, but affect the other soldiers returning, as well." She looked up at her friend and smiled. "I'm sorry that it's been so rough. You were amazing, and I'm so glad that you took this challenge with me. Do you have any thoughts that I should bring to the King? Any ideas for solutions?"

"Give them a purpose. Right now, that's all they are really asking for. A sense of direction. Find a few from the ranks who you can promote to help keep things in order, and discuss with the king what his plans are for dealing with the trauma of all of this. I do have books in my library that discuss treatments for the mental afflictions of returned soldiers. It's not uncommon for them to have issues adjusting to being home after what they've dealt with, even under normal circumstances. Much of the necessary treatment is discussing and working through things with a guide who helps them through troubling memories and emotions."

"Dwarves have those sorts of treatments?"

An image of the small but burly men sitting around and talking about their feelings popped into Adalyn's head. It seemed so completely against the aggressive mannerisms she has seen from the dwarven society so far.

"No, not dwarves. The elves. It's part of how they keep their society so refined. Maybe you can discuss it with Venlian when you return. By the way, how long are you going to be here?"

"Only a few days. I promise to check in more frequently now that I know that I can."

The relief on Eridu's face was evident. "I would appreciate that. I won't keep you longer right now. If you need me, you know where I will be."

Adalyn rose and shared one last smile before exiting the office.

As Glenda and Adalyn worked their way upward from the underground Banneret halls, she processed everything that she had just seen. She had never been responsible for another person, let alone a bunch of other people, and suddenly she was saddled with life changing decisions.

"Glenda, what all did the Banneret do before the war?"

"While we were our own unit, we really filled out the rest of the services in the castle. Our abilities are unique to each member, and no single purpose would utilize them properly."

A servant carrying an armload of firewood approached them and Adalyn waited for her to pass before continuing to speak.

"What sort of things?

"Those who had healing abilities served as part of the king's medical care. A few stayed here, but most traveled around the kingdom healing those they could."

"I could see that being beneficial. If you had a good king who sent them through the entire kingdom, it would foster good will among the people. Especially if illness broke out. Were they paid as a part of the Banneret, or did they charge the people they served?"

"It depended on the king. Usually they received free food and lodging as they traveled."

Another pair of servants walked towards them carrying buckets and tools to clear out the fireplaces. Adalyn waited again for them to pass before continuing so as to not raise suspicion by talking to herself.

"What did the Banneret who didn't have healing abilities do?"

"Those good with animals helped where they could. Some who could connect with the earth traveled and encouraged the crops during the growing season. Shapeshifters and mind melders often worked as spies or in theater troops. Truth tellers were ambassadors, while those who are telepathic were stationed all over the kingdom and often in other kingdoms to speed up communication. Others helped fill out the ranks of soldiers and historians."

"I had no idea there were so many different abilities."

"There's many more. Not everyone with abilities joined or stayed in the Banneret, but those who did, did it to be useful. These past two months they've felt anything but."

Adalyn considered Glenda's words as they made their way through busier hallways and up to the king's study. It was still early enough in the day that his meetings shouldn't have started yet, and Adalyn hoped that she could have this discussion with him before a crowd was there to participate as well. Pausing in front of the door, she straightened her uniform and knocked as steadily as she could with her shaking hands.

"Come in."

Opening the door, Adalyn was relieved to find the king alone.

A smile spread across his young face. "You're back."

She performed a quick bow and spoke as she rose. "I am. I won't be here very long, but due to the time difference, I can stay for a day or two. I'm working on a way to be here more often for when you need me."

King Coeus nodded his head. "I understand. Things hadn't been so complicated, but as more soldiers returned from both the Banneret and army, we've been putting out fires while we figure out what to do. There were so many more soldiers left over there than we'd thought."

"From what I've heard, there are many more to come."

"I think you're right. While you're here, let's discuss what to do with the Banneret. I've heard they are getting a bit rough downstairs."

Adalyn laughed. "That's one way to put it. They're

bored, lonely, and honestly, sad. Everything they were fighting for is gone."

"I understand. I'm seeing it with the traditional troops, as well. Currently the scuffles have stayed within our ranks, but I'm afraid it won't be too long until that is no longer the case."

"Have you discussed this with Eridu?"

"Some. I was planning on meeting with her soon if you didn't arrive."

"She has some ideas about ways to help the anger and depression. I will discuss with Venlian what she was telling me, but apparently the elves have developed a way to help their people acclimate to their new lives after wars."

King Coeus stroked his beard and leaned back in his chair. "Really? I will have her added to the agenda for a private meeting. If you could discuss it with him and see if we could get more information, or even help, from the elves, it would be appreciated."

"Of course. I also had another thought."

"Go ahead."

"Before the war, the Banneret were used by the kings to help support and reach his goodwill out to all of the kingdom. Perhaps you can do this again. It would give them the opportunity to have a purpose again. Obviously, they would need to earn your trust to be allowed to travel like this, but it may help them integrate into the kingdom's population now."

"I think that's a good idea. Do you have specific suggestions?"

"I can write them up and send them to you later today."

"Please do. How are things going in Chors?"

"I think we're making progress," Adalyn said with a sigh. "It's only been a few days, and we are still trapped in the castle under suspicion…"

The king leaned forward suddenly. "You're *what?*"

"While the validity of our letters and claims is being proven, we are restricted to the castle. I understand, and they have been kind enough to give us a guest suite and freedom to travel around the castle grounds accompanied."

"They dare do that to the ambassadors I sent?" King Coeus's fists shook as his voice rose. "They dare to ignore facts not only from me, but from other royalty, as well?"

Adalyn felt herself shrink a bit. "I'm sure it's not personal. King Garren doesn't know any of us personally, and when we arrived, he thought we were still at war. From what I saw at my last visit with him, he seemed to be leaning towards believing us. Actually, you sent the right people to come get me."

He took a deep breath. "Really? How so?"

"One of the golems you sent is an old friend of the king's."

Resting his elbows on the arms of his chair, King Coeus clasped his hands in front of his face and slowly nodded while he thought. "Good, I'm glad."

Not sure what else to add, Adalyn shifted on her feet for a few moments until a knock sounded at the door.

The king looked up suddenly as if broken from a trance. "Come in."

A weaselly man peeked his head through the door. "We are ready for you, your highness."

"I will be there momentarily," King Coeus responded with a wave of his hand.

The door quietly closed as the man retreated, and the king redirected his attention to Adalyn. "Do you have anything else to report?"

"Nothing else to report; we've only been there a few days. I do have a thought, though. Have you met Banneret Brinn?"

"The name is familiar."

"I would like to promote him to a position directly under Eridu to help her organize the Banneret and keep them in line."

"Do you trust him?"

"The brief encounter I've had with him told me that he is upright, willing to listen, not hostile towards my position, and that he has the respect of his men."

King Coeus nodded once. "I leave that judgment up to you. If you want him to be promoted, just fill out the paperwork and have Eridu submit it before you leave."

"Will do. Thank you. That's everything." She hesitated awkwardly as she partially bowed while starting to leave, before stopping herself as she realized that she hadn't been dismissed yet.

He chuckled. "You're free to go. Thank you, and please visit us when you can."

She nodded and quickly left the room, her face burning from embarrassment. Her stomach growled as she contemplated what to do next. It seemed to have decided for her, and she could only hope that a certain someone stuck around and would be there, as well.

CHAPTER SEVEN

The smell of fresh baked bread told Adalyn that she was getting to the kitchen just in time for one of her favorite days of the week. The bread was made once a week, and if you caught it fresh out of the oven, there was nothing better. Not even chocolate from the Guppy Sweets shop or the coffee from Maggie's Inn. Both were favorites of hers, and both businesses that she wasn't sure were even still around. The thought saddened her a bit, but the image of the crunch from the crust of the bread softened the blow.

Entering the kitchen, she looked for friendly faces. There were fewer than she had hoped and more than she'd feared. Really, her time in the castle before leaving for Chors after the battle to retake the capital had been brief and busy. She didn't know just who had survived from the kitchen.

Adalyn heard a familiar voice from a flour-covered redhead. "I see you decided to grace us with your presence, your fancy-pants-ness."

A laugh erupted from Adalyn as she walked over to greet her best friend. "Never too fancy for you. Just busy."

Isabella gave her a knowing grin. "I've heard. I'm glad you're here, though."

"I'm not here for long, only a day or two. I have to get things in order before heading back to Chors."

"So soon?"

"Technically, they don't know I'm gone, so I probably should get back soon."

"I understand. I'm glad you found time to stop by and say hi."

Adalyn gestured towards the bread on the table in front of them. "I'm here for a bit more than to just say hi."

This time Isabella was the one who laughed. "Of course, you are. Come, sit down. Fill me in on all of the details while you eat."

Pulling up a stool, Adalyn did just that, sharing as much as she was permitted.

"That's crazy! You're stuck in the castle?"

Dramatically raising her hands up in front of her with a twist of her wrists, Adalyn smirked. "I'm not as trapped as everyone thinks I am."

Isabella laughed. "I've missed your sass."

"Yeah, life has been too serious for the last while. I've missed that version of me, too." Adalyn dropped her hands to her side and felt herself deflate a bit when she thought about what she had left behind in Chors.

Taking note of the change in demeanor, Isabella asked, "Is it that much of a burden?"

"No, not really."

"Then what is it?"

Knowing that she needed to discuss it with someone, Adalyn quietly started talking, though she couldn't bring herself to look at her friend as she did so. "Do you remember me telling you about Bevin?"

"Yeah, the girl from the village that went to meet the king with you."

"That's her. Really, she's great, but I'm not sure if I'm feeling jealous, or worried…"

Isabella leaned on her elbows on the table. "Why would you feel that?"

Adalyn heaved a sigh. "I just thought that Nolan and I were sort of a thing."

"You two are very cute together. What did he do?"

Her hands free of bread, Adalyn started fidgeting with her hands. "Nothing, really. We just haven't had much time together since heading back to Chors, and I saw him helping Bevin while training. I mean, it wasn't like they were really doing anything wrong. I just… I don't…" Adalyn let out a frustrated grunt. "I don't know. I'm overthinking nothing."

"You're not that kind of person, Adalyn. You're loyal and tend to have a good read on people. It's all right that you don't know what exactly is going on, but wouldn't talking to them about it be the best solution?"

"True. I haven't had the chance yet. I haven't seen them since I *saw* them. I'm sure it's nothing. Never mind."

"When you get back, just take a moment to check in. While you two weren't technically in an official relationship as far as I know, you were being exclusive to him."

"Not that I had any opportunity elsewise, but yes. I've been exclusive to him. I really like him."

"Can you picture yourself joining their caravan?"

Adalyn didn't respond.

"You don't know. You haven't really thought this through, yet, have you? I know you said that you two had talked about it, but that was before you were captain of the Banneret."

Silence was Adalyn's response again.

"No worries, you've got time. Besides, if it doesn't work out, you can consider your other option. Nolan wasn't the only interested party."

"Excuse me?" Adalyn's aversion to looking at her friend suddenly disappeared, and she searched Isabella's face intently.

"Oh, come on, you really never got those vibes from Venlian?"

Adalyn's cheeks started burning again.

"You did! Or maybe you just hope that's the case?"

"Maybe? There were a few moments, but Nolan was my focus. I didn't read into them or anything."

Isabella snorted. "Apparently so. What moments?"

Flashes of small interactions flashed through Adalyn's head. Being tucked into the chair in his library when she knew she hadn't had a blanket before. His attention while at Bevin's sister's wedding. And the book... just what had that book said that made him decide he needed to be part of her life?

Choosing to keep the memories to herself, she only replied, "Just small things. How about you? How have things been here since we took back the capital?"

Isabella pulled a chunk of dough from a large bowl

and began kneading it with her hands and tying it into a small knot.

"Things have been really good. Very quiet, which is a nice change after the last while. Glen took over for Chef down here, and you probably noticed the new staff."

Adalyn took another bite of her crusty bread and let out a happy sigh. "I did. It looks like things are running smoothly. Did you do something different to this bread?"

"Glen changed the recipe a bit. That one has rosemary and garlic added to the loaf."

"This has to be…" Adalyn paused after noting that a few of the precious crumbs were spraying out of her mouth as she spoke. "This has to be the best bread that I've ever had."

Isabella pointed back at the fireplace where Glen stood. "Tell him, he's been obsessing over getting things as good as he can. We use Chef's original recipes, but they're all getting updated."

Adalyn's heart clenched as she looked at Glen. He was really a great guy, but the wound from Chef's betrayal was still there. He had practically been her family for so many years.

Noticing the change in Adalyn's face, Isabella placed her hand on Adalyn's sleeve, leaving a faint print of white dust. "I'm sorry. I forget that you haven't had the same time to grieve that we have."

Adalyn took a deep breath to settle her nerves. "It's all right. I know what he did, and I will process it eventually."

"It's okay to mourn the loss of someone who had been such a big part of your life, though."

Adalyn nodded while taking another bite, burying her emotions in comfort food while too close to tears to speak.

"Oh! I haven't told you the good news yet! I met someone."

Taking another deep breath, Adalyn pasted on a faint smile, glad for the distraction. "You did?"

The grin on Isabella's face stretched from ear to ear. She practically bounced where she stood. "Yep! He's actually one of your men."

"It's going to take a while for me to get used to the idea that I have people I'm responsible for. Who is it?"

"His name is Brinn. He's sweet, he's charming, and most importantly, really, really cute."

"How did you happen to fall for one of the only Banneret that I have actually met?"

"So you know him?" Isabella's hands flew up in excitement, tossing a cloud of white behind her, which another cook choked on. "Sorry, I didn't mean to do that."

With rolled eyes and a smile, the cook went back to work. Remembering what it was like to work in the same kitchen as Isabella, Adalyn figured this wasn't the first time this had happened.

"I do know him. Only a little, though. I'm actually going to look for him next."

"Oh! Want to bring him a little care package from your favorite kitchen help?"

Adalyn couldn't help but feel a bit of the excitement rubbing off from her friend. "I can do that. I just have to figure out where to find him."

"That's easy. Mornings, he trains with the sword masters. Really, he is very, very good. You sit there and finish your food, and I will put this together for you to take. Eek! I'm so excited. What a good start to the day!"

ADALYN STOOD ON THE EDGE OF THE TRAINING grounds and watched the men spar. The last time she had been here was when Chors attacked. So much had changed.

Sure, it was the same stone walls and hardened dirt ground. The same smell of sweat and blood, and the sound of yells and clashing metal. Everything else had changed, though. The marks on the walls showed the battle that had raged in this courtyard. The arms master and his soldiers who had trained with her were all gone.

A voice shook her from her sad reminiscing. "Sam, Drak, you guys are up next. Silver only, and first red wins."

Completely confused, Adalyn nudged another watcher nearby. "What did he just say?"

The man gave her a once over. "Are you new here? Silver means real blades only, and first red means first blood drawn."

"Wait, they're actually doing this until they physically hurt each other?"

He shrugged. "It's no different than using wooden weapons. I would much rather have a small cut than the battered bruises from a wooden sword."

Adalyn nodded as she realized that she would also choose the same. She watched as the two men expertly slashed at one another while dodging dangerous blows.

Finally, one raised his hand to show a small cut on the top of his wrist, and the fight was over.

The two men shook hands and melted back into the watching crowd. All other sparring had ceased as people gathered to watch the duels.

"Jacob and Triston, you are…Captain! You're here!"

The crowd followed his line of sight and parted in front of Adalyn, leaving her feeling very exposed.

"Brinn, it's good to see you." Adalyn walked over to join him. "I'm only here for a short while before heading back to Chors to work on negotiations."

"We understand. If anyone knows just how desperately we need this truce, it's those of us who came from Chors after you showed up."

A chorus of agreement surrounded them.

"Are you here for business or pleasure? Want to join?"

"Oh, no, as much fun as that sounds, I can promise you that I am undertrained for the level that you all are fighting at." The fact that that statement may bite her in the behind later crossed her mind, but she chose not to care.

"So be it. Jacob, Triston, you're up. Silvers only, and first to draw red."

Adalyn and Brinn backed into the crowd and watched the two begin to spar.

"I come bearing a care package."

Brinn gave her a quizzical look until he saw the cloth-wrapped package tied with kitchen string. "You saw Isabella?"

"She's a good friend."

He took the package from her and tucked it under his

arm. "Oh, I've heard. She only has good things to say about you."

"And I, her. She is a pretty incredible friend. I do have a question—where are the rest of the soldiers? I know that only a very small number can fit in here to train. Even just the Banneret have to be more than this."

"Only the elite and fulltime soldiers use this training area. The rest are camped outside the city, booked into the inns, and fill up every chamber available in the castle. Most were conscripted and have no desire to stay soldiers. They just don't have anything to go back to."

"That makes sense. How many Banneret are back so far?"

"As of yesterday, I think around three-hundred forty-six."

Adalyn's eyes grew wide. "That many? Are some of them camped outside the city, as well?"

"The Banneret halls below the mountain are vast. We still have room for several hundred more as they return or are called."

"Wait, what do you mean, called?"

"That's how most Banneret join the ranks. Many had abilities, but not everyone felt the need to join. Usually if an item came into their possession, they joined up eventually. I knew, personally, once I found this beauty." Brinn tapped a dagger on his waist. "I had this nagging in my mind telling me that I needed to come here."

"I had no idea. Have we had others show up besides the ones returning from Chors?"

He nodded. "We just had someone show up a few

days ago. I have a feeling that it is going to start happening more frequently now that magic has returned to Pieriun."

Adalyn thought about everything that he had just told her. Just how much she didn't know was becoming very apparent to her. She knew that he was exactly who she needed to work with Eridu to make sense of all of this.

"Brinn, I have a proposition for you."

"I'm all ears."

"I want to promote you to lieutenant and have you work directly with Eridu while I'm in Chors. I need someone who can help organize things who has the experience and knowledge necessary, and who I can personally trust."

Brinn stared at her. "Are you serious?"

"Absolutely. I can continue my list of reasons why I want you instead of someone else if you need."

"No need. I'm just surprised. This may ruffle some feathers."

"It will also help smooth quite a few, as well. Any others will adapt over time."

He looked around the crowd as if considering his options, his eyes resting on the still-sparring pair. "All right, I accept. The men do need someone who has the experience."

"I agree. Eridu has some ideas to help get the ball rolling, but I'm going to be relying heavily on you while I'm gone."

"Understood. Thank you."

A small but very deep yelp drew Brinn's attention back to the sparring pair. One of the men held his thigh. "Congratulations, Triston. Who wants to go next and show just how valuable they can be to our captain?"

Adalyn was shocked to see so many hands shoot into the air all at once. While she was starting to understand her role, she still didn't feel very important. Maybe that was part of the problem. Maybe she had lived so much of her life as just a participant that she hadn't taken the chance to learn how to actively control what happened. Maybe that needed to change.

CHAPTER EIGHT

A wave of exhaustion hit her as she returned to her room in Chors, and Adalyn struggled to sit on the edge of her bed. The strain of making her magic work as she forced her way through the weakened but still potent spell took everything out of her.

Knowing that she still had a few hours before the sun would begin to rise, she decided to get a glass of water before giving in to her exhaustion under those sumptuous covers. She walked quietly out her door and paused when she saw movement in the sitting room.

The light flickering off Venlian's silver hair gave the appearance of a halo around his head as he sat before the fire, and the sight made Adalyn's breath catch. The sound made his gaze dart up from the book he was reading and fix on her.

"I'm sorry. I'm just getting a drink and heading to bed." Adalyn turned and hurried over to the table to pour herself a glass of water as Venlian stood and approached her. She drank, gulping faster with each footstep as he got closer to her.

"I was actually waiting for you."

She nearly choked on her next gulp, splashing water as she lowered the glass.

"You were?"

He nodded, watching as she wiped water from her chin. Why did she have to be so awkward?

"Thank you," she said. "I'm all right. Exhausted, but it's been a busy few days, and that living spell is still so incredibly strong."

"I was afraid of that. Were you able to do everything you needed to while you were there?"

Setting the glass back down, Adalyn leaned on the table behind her. "I think so. I got the most important stuff at least started in the right direction to get fixed. I will head back tomorrow night and check in on things. Oh! Before I forget—Eridu found a record about some treatment that the elves have for soldiers who return from war. She wanted me to ask you about it."

"We do have something in place. I'm not sure how much help it will be, but I can write a letter and have you deliver it to my people on your way back to Pieriun. I can't promise that they will agree, but I can ask them personally to help."

"Thank you, that would be very much appreciated," Adalyn said, offering a weak smile that was disrupted by a jaw-popping yawn. "I'm so sorry. I'm going to head to bed. Is it all right if we continue this discussion tomorrow?"

Venlian stepped aside. "Of course. Sleep well."

Covering another yawn with her hand she walked back towards her room. "You, too."

The main room was empty when Adalyn awoke. Not surprising, considering she had slept well into the morning. She grabbed a biscuit from a basket that had been left on the table and wandered towards the door to outside.

A gust of fresh air brushed her loose hair across her face as she stepped onto the enclosed balcony. The cool stone of the railing felt refreshing under her fingertips in the sticky air.

As she took a large bite of the buttery biscuit, something moving in the shadows below caught her attention. She peered into the courtyard below, her interest piqued. Flowers and bushes bloomed along grassy paths, creating a small maze. Gates stood at opposite ends of the courtyard, and pillars lined the edges, supporting the balconies above.

Movement in her periphery further down the courtyard pulled her gaze, but she couldn't see anything when she looked in that direction.

Still feeling a bit worn from using her ability the night before, Adalyn shoved the rest of the biscuit in her mouth and glanced around to check if she was alone. Eyeing the pillar next to where she had last seen movement, she worldwalked across and stepped behind the pillar.

She was slightly disappointed and very confused at finding nothing there.

Adalyn whipped her head towards a small scuffling

sound further down the shadows and saw something only for a moment. Feeling like a hound on the hunt, she worldwalked to that point, only to be disappointed again.

The gate in front of her creaked, and a cloak corner whipped around it just as she looked.

Glancing around to make sure she was unobserved, Adalyn hurried to the gate and peered through the crack between it and the wall. Deciding all was clear, she world-walked to the other side of the wall.

She looked around the large open area there, but saw nothing. She waited a few minutes in case she could catch sight of anything of interest, but whoever she was following had completely vanished. Anxious about getting caught without an escort, she prepared to worldwalk back to her suite, only to hear a familiar pair of voices getting closer.

"It has been several hundred years since we saw each other last."

"For you, it has. For me it's only been a few months." The feminine voice had an edge to it that told Adalyn the speaker was struggling to control her emotions.

"I understand that. I'm not who I was then, though. I'm old enough to be your father at this point."

Adalyn ducked behind a nearby bush at the realization that she was overhearing a private conversation between Venlian and Sariah. While she knew that she should just worldwalk back to her room, she wanted to hear how this would end. She hated it when her curiosity won over her common sense, but her heart wanted her to stay.

Sariah scoffed. "That means nothing to our people, and you know it."

"It means something to me."

"What are you saying, then?"

"You know exactly what I'm saying."

Their footsteps stopped one after the other, and the silence lasted for what felt like forever.

"I was broken for a long time, and have only recently found a new light in my life. I'm sure that you will find the same for yourself someday." Venlian's voice sounded strained.

"You can't take this back later. You know that, right?"

"I know. I won't need to."

Adalyn could hear the sarcasm dripping from Sariah's short laugh. "Did your books tell you that?"

Silence once again.

"Wait, they did? Are you serious?"

"You know how the books work. I didn't finish reading it."

"Half of the time other races think we are all-knowing, it's because of those stupid books."

Venlian's laugh cut through the tension. "That, and because we live a ridiculously long time."

Sariah chuckled. "Very true."

Silence for a moment again.

"I'll miss you."

"It's not like I'm dying."

"You know what I mean."

"You know what I mean, as well."

Adalyn's leg cramped, and a twig broke under her foot as she shifted to ease it.

Venlian's voice reverted back to his more serious tone. "We should head back."

Worried that she would be caught, Adalyn decided not to delay any longer and worldwalked back to the guest suite. Kicking herself for not having gone to her room specifically, she was relieved to find the main room empty. She picked up a random book from the shelves and sat down, trying to look occupied in case they were coming back to the suite.

A history of Almendra. Half tempted to put it back, Adalyn cracked the spine open to take a peek and immediately felt the pull of her ability towards the book.

What was wrong with her? Since when could she not read a book without her ability trying to make her connect with it and drag her in? She grudgingly surrendered and watched as a city of white stone and copper-domed roofs appeared around her. The age of the buildings was apparent by the amount of patina and lichen that had developed on most of the homes. Water seemed to be everywhere. Rivulets trickled down buildings into elaborate pools and fountains, and Adalyn was awestruck by the time and dedication this engineering marvel must have taken.

The mumblings of a crowd quickly grew as the scene became clear. Everything, from the buildings to the jewelry and cloth that people wore, screamed wealth. Much of it was made from materials that her own merchant parents never let her handle as a child because it was too valuable and easily marked.

The smell of cloves and ash hit her nose and drew her attention towards a single person, a woman whose dark hair and green eyes looked familiar, though she couldn't quite place why. Curious, Adalyn followed the woman from market stall to market stall as she bought a variety of ingredients, including ones that were not out on display.

The woman tucked each parcel inside her cloak as she made her way down the street. The crowd parted as she passed, many nodding a hello or offering a greeting, which the woman always returned.

"Gathering supplies for my husband's tonic?" The soft female voice made both Adalyn and the woman she had been following jump.

The woman quickly bowed. "I am, my queen. It should be ready by this evening."

Curious, Adalyn looked the queen over. Soft white strands snuck out of her braided bun and blew in the wind. She looked neither young nor old, and had an almost mystical quality about her.

"Thank you. He's having a rather rough day today. The weather getting colder always makes his condition worse, and each winter is more difficult for him." Only love and concern showed in the woman's eyes. Adalyn couldn't help but admire and wonder what kind of queen she must have been.

"I will be on, then. I have several hours of work ahead of me to get this ready." The cloaked woman bowed deeply again and headed back into the crowd.

Adalyn was tempted to follow the queen and see why she was at the market, but something about the cloaked woman was nagging her in the back of her mind. She hurried to catch up and continued to follow her through a series of alleys until they eventually reached a heavy wooden door.

An equally heavy key was pulled from the cloak, and

with a quick glance around, the woman entered and latched the door behind her. Adalyn stepped through the closed door to find the woman laying out her parcels on a table in a rather simple room. A flick of the fingers had a roaring fire going in the hearth, a large cauldron hanging over it. Narrow shelves with books and bottles hung on the walls, and a basket with cooking utensils sat on a large platter.

The woman removed her cloak and hung it on a hook on the wall. She began to remove bottles from the shelves and pull things from the dried plants hanging from the ceiling. Muttering to herself, she cut things up and tossed them into the cauldron.

Mesmerized, Adalyn lost track of time entirely. The smell that filled the room told her that either this woman was a terrible cook, or she wasn't making anything meant to be eaten.

The women stood in front of the fire and stirred, quietly counting under her breath, starting over again as she switched which direction she stirred.

Suddenly, she stopped, pulled a copper mug from her belt, and dipped it in the cauldron. She closed her eyes as she brought the mug to her lips and took in a deep breath.

Adalyn's breath caught as she watched the woman drain the entire mug, anxious to see the effects of the foul liquid.

A clang rang out in the small room as the mug fell and hit the stone floor. The woman clenched her throat and let out a groan as she shrank towards the floor.

A heavy mist poured out of the cauldron and became so thick that Adalyn couldn't see what was happening.

Chills ran down her spine at the non-human whimpers and snarls coming from where the woman had been.

Moments later, cries could be heard outside. The screams multiplied and were joined by sounds of chaos.

Adalyn rushed out, a horrible sight greeting her as soon as she walked through the wall.

Monsters, hideous creatures, filled the streets, attacking each other seemingly at random. The mist from inside passed through the door as if it didn't exist and was carried down the street by the wind. She expected to see people rushing to safety, but saw no one at all as she made her way back to the marketplace. the scene there was much the same, beasts tearing each other limb from limb.

A hand on her shoulder startled her, and in the blink of an eye she was back in the guest suite, sitting on a chair, gasping, with the book in her hands. It no longer called to her ability as it had before.

"I'm sorry, I didn't mean to alarm you."

Adalyn looked up at Venlian, his hand still on her shoulder.

"I take it it's a good book?"

"That's one way to put it."

She closed the book and shifted, feeling tension run through her body from what she had just witnessed. As she remembered why she was holding the book to begin with, the conversation she had overheard earlier popped into her mind. Adalyn rolled her shoulders, effectively wiggling the one out from under Venlian's hand.

"Can I help you?" she asked.

He searched her face, trying to figure out what he had

interrupted, and why it had made her so stiff. "I was sent to deliver this."

Adalyn took the note from his outstretched hand. She popped the seal and opened it to expose a very delicate cursive scrawled across the page.

Captain Adalyn Mernt,

You have been invited to afternoon tea with Queen Faith at two past the crest this afternoon. Your guards will escort you to the designated location.

She read the invitation several times before looking up at Venlian.

"Who gave you this? There's no signature."

"One of the guards handed it to me as I returned. Is there a problem?"

Adalyn handed him the parchment and allowed him to read it for himself.

"Do you want me to come with you?"

She shook her head. "No, the invitation was only extended to me. Um, when exactly is two past the crest?"

"Two in the afternoon."

She nodded as she processed that. "And, what time is it now?"

"It's one."

The book hit the floor as she suddenly stood. "I've got to get ready! I need to fix my hair, and get dressed…"

Adalyn looked down at the dirt on the knees of her leathers. "You don't happen to know what one is supposed to wear to tea with the queen of Chors five hundred years ago, do you?"

Venlian chuckled. "Come on, let's get you ready. Go wash up, and I'll help you find something suitable. If that's all right with you, that is."

"Please do!"

Adalyn picked up the book and replaced it on the shelf, allowing herself only the briefest moment to ponder what she'd seen inside it before hurrying to get ready for what she was sure would be the least comfortable tea she had ever been to.

CHAPTER NINE

With minimal fussing, Adalyn stood in front of her mirror tying a leather cord on the end of her freshly braided hair. They had decided on a clean dress uniform—formal, yet as comfortable as she could get for such an occasion. She paused for a moment to admire in the mirror how the blue wool of the jacket somehow made her eyes pop. She buttoned the last brass button and turned to ensure that nothing was out of place. Deciding that this was as good as it was going to get, she took a deep breath and opened the door of her room to find a small—er, *large*—crowd had gathered in their sitting room.

"You look beautiful, my dear," Lazuli said as she approached Adalyn. "Truly beautiful. No need to be nervous; Queen Faith is one of the good ones."

"As good as any power-hungry royal can be," Carnelian spat.

Merit smacked Carnelian over the head with a loud thunk. "Watch your mouth! You can easily lose your keystone talking like that." He turned to Adalyn. "Lazuli is right. You have nothing to worry about. Queen Faith has always been one to see things as they are. She's not aggressive, but waits for the right time to act. You'll be fine."

Adalyn chuckled nervously. "Thanks, guys. I wasn't expecting you all to be here."

"We figured we would check in with you after your trip," Iolite said, "but that can wait until after you return."

"Of course. I will do that after I get back. I should get going, though. It's never smart to keep a queen waiting."

Adalyn started towards the door, just to stop as Venlian stepped in front and opened it for her.

"Be safe. Be smart," he said. "We are still in negotiations."

"I will. Thank you."

With one last look, she stepped out of the room and motioned to the guards outside that she was ready to leave.

Adalyn was completely lost after only a few turns. Hallway after hallway and courtyard after courtyard, she followed her escort until they finally stopped in front of a thick wooden door. Her guard knocked three times and stepped back.

It opened to reveal a skinny young woman, who gave the group a once over. "May I help you?"

"I'm Adalyn Mernt. Queen Faith invited me."

The door opened wider, and with a gesture of her arm, the young woman welcomed Adalyn. "Of course! This way, if you please."

White with gold details adorned the furniture and fabrics of the room. No art hung from the stone walls, only mirrors in gilt frames. Adalyn followed the woman through the room and out into a small, walled garden.

"Captain Adalyn Mernt, your majesty," the woman announced.

Adalyn bowed before she could take in more than the bright red hair piled on top of the Queen Faith's head. As she waited to be acknowledged so she could rise, she glimpsed a pair of green satin slippers peeking out from under the hem of a green and white dress.

"It's wonderful to finally meet you, Adalyn Mernt. Please join me," a firm but kind voice commanded.

Adalyn rose quickly and took the seat opposite the queen at a small table filled with the most ornate pastries she had ever seen. Her mouth immediately began watering as the smells of apricot and almond hit her nose.

"You've stirred up quite a fuss with your arrival."

"I promise, no fuss was intended. We just want our kingdoms to be at peace," Adalyn replied, quickly adding, "your majesty."

The servant poured tea for both women, and Adalyn added two large spoons of sugar and took a drink.

A smile spread across the Queen's face. "As do I. Tell me, what abilities do you have?"

Tea sprayed out of Adalyn's nose.

"Oh my goodness! I'm so sorry!" Adalyn blurted as she grabbed her napkin to wipe things up.

The queen broke out in laughter, and Adalyn glanced back and forth between her and the maid, who was helping clean up, watching to see if this was a good thing or not.

"That was the last reaction I expected, Queen Faith

said, wiping tears from her eyes. "Is this not something that is openly spoken about in Pieriun? You are the captain of the Banneret, are you not?"

"Yes, your majesty, I am. Pieriun has changed quite a bit from when you may have last seen it. I was just surprised."

"Ah, I see. Please, continue. I want to hear all about these changes."

Adalyn gave a brief history of Pieriun since the living spell had been cast and the events that led her to Chors. The queen asked a few questions between sips of tea.

Placing her gold-trimmed cup on its saucer, Queen Faith asked, "So your people are now afraid of magic? That's why you reacted so when I asked about your abilities?"

"Yes," Adalyn replied, looking down at her hands and mentally kicking herself again for spraying the queen with tea. "I'm so terribly sorry about that."

The Queen was silent for a moment. "Please don't think of it any longer. You've done nothing wrong, and I entirely understand the cause of it now."

"Thank you."

"May I ask what you personally hope to get out of this alliance?"

Adalyn thought about it. No one had asked her this before.

"Peace," she answered. "I've gone from being a merchant's daughter with modest means to homeless. I've had great joy and pain in my life. I had a simple life as one of the king's cooks, and I only want that contentment in my life again. It wouldn't have to be as a cook, necessarily, but I know that as long as our kingdoms are still at war, I will never get that again."

"Do you think you will get that as a Banneret?"

"I doubt it. I took the position because there was no one else who could. Once things have been sorted out, I can take the time to decide what my next step is."

"You're wise for someone so young."

"I often feel older than my actual age."

The queen nodded. "And what do you think of Chors?"

"I think the people are good. I can see why our two kingdoms chose to unite with a marriage. I'm ashamed, as I think most of the people of Pieriun are, about how this war escalated. When I learned of how mad our king had become, I felt only sadness."

"The fault for the war isn't entirely on your kingdom. We certainly had our part to play. I'm sure you've heard of my son's mistress."

"I have. I haven't met her, but I've heard of her part in it."

"Did you know that she is the true cause of this war? The way the men listen to her every whim makes me wonder if she is a sorceress or enchantress. I've looked into it, of course. I just haven't found anything."

"I'd heard she was the reason our princess returned home. She was insulted by something and swore revenge."

"That's one way to put it. My son's mistress convinced him that they should have a child and that this child should be the heir, making Princess Morgan's marriage practically pointless. My son spends more time with that woman than he did with her. I'm afraid I couldn't do anything to help her. My husband also seems entranced, and I hardly see him or my son anymore."

"I'm sorry this all happened."

"No need to be sorry. While your past is my present, I see that you at least hold no ill will towards our people. May I ask you a favor?"

"Certainly."

"Be careful of my son's mistress. Don't seek her out, but when you do meet her, be wary. Be mindful and listen to your instincts. I have no magical abilities, but perhaps you can sense something that I cannot."

"I will do that. I promise."

"Thank you. In return, I will speak with my husband regarding an alliance. While I may not always have his ear, I have my ways of making him listen."

Adalyn smiled. "That would be wonderful."

The two of them continued to talk while snacking on some of the most delicious desserts Adalyn had ever eaten for another hour. Adalyn adjusted the waist of her pants as she walked back to her room with her escort, trying to relieve the pressure on her very content stomach. She opened her door to an even larger crowd than she had left.

"Did you bring me any left overs?" Carnelian, the first to notice she had arrived, asked.

"Do golems even eat?"

He chuckled. "Not really, but the thought would have been nice."

"Now, Carnelian, you can't give her a hard time like that. How did it go, dear?" Lazuli asked.

"Rather well, I think."

Adalyn walked over to join the group and found only

two seats available. She could either sit by Venlian on one couch or squeeze in next to Nolan and Bevin on the other. The golems had taken over all of the chairs, which groaned in protest with each move they made. Adalyn took the place beside Venlian.

A small smile formed on Venlian's face before he spoke. "Did you find out why she wanted to speak with you?"

"Something about the prince's mistress. She warned me about her and asked if I could see if my ability felt anything strange."

"Yeah, she has a reputation throughout the kingdom," Bevin piped in. "Most people avoid her until they actually meet her."

"What does that mean?" Nolan said, turning to face Bevin.

"She's right," Iolite said. "This mistress showed up out of nowhere. No one knows where she is from, but everything started falling apart after she showed up. People traveled to bring their concerns to the king and returned with their minds completely changed, ready to go to war."

"The queen said something similar. She did mention that it's the men, though, not the women who are manipulated. Have you ever met her, Merit?"

"Only once, just after I became a golem. I accompanied my brothers to try and stop the war, but it's as they've said. They all changed their minds."

Venlian tilted his head. "Why were you not affected?"

"I don't know. Perhaps because I'm no longer flesh and blood? Maybe whatever enchantment she's using only affects mortals."

Everyone in the room nodded as they processed the information.

Adalyn sat up suddenly. "Wait, your family is still alive?"

"Of course. Why wouldn't they be?"

"I guess I just assumed that you all had lived long lives as golems."

"We have," Lazuli replied. "Merit is the youngest of the golems who went to Pieriun, but he was there all those years ago. He's lived the lifetime of many dwarves."

"What about you?"

"Ah, a lady never tells."

"She's a thousand two-hundred sixty-two."

A fluttering of pages was followed by a soft thunk as Lazuli threw a large book at Carnelian. "Hush, you fool. It's not your place to tell. I outrank you, remember?"

"Only because you've been a golem a hundred years longer than I."

Adalyn had thought they had to be old, but didn't expect these kinds of numbers. "What about you, Iolite?"

Carnelian spoke before Iolite could. "He's an original."

Adalyn's jaw dropped. "Truly?"

"I am. I was one of the first, but I've lost track too many times for me to know my own age."

"That's incredible! I'm curious; I know that Merit was a prince before he became a golem." Adalyn pointed her finger at her pearlescent golem friend. "I don't know what the rest of you did, though. Did you ask to become golems?"

"I was a bard," Carnelian said.

Adalyn, Nolan, and Bevin laughed.

Nolan was the first to bring himself to stop. "Excuse me? You were a bard? Somehow I can't picture that."

Arms crossed, Carnelian leaned back in his chair and tilted his chin up. "I was one of the most sought-after bards of my time. In fact, I was given the opportunity to become a golem because I followed my king's men into battle and was one of the few to return. I wrote the song that holds the memory of that war and those we lost. It's still sung today."

"That's amazing," Bevin said. "Would you sing it for us?"

Carnelian shifted uncomfortably.

"He claims he forgot the words in his old age," Merit teased.

"That's not it! My voice carried over to this body, but it's not the same."

Adalyn wiped the tears from her eyes as she finally finished chuckling. "I'm so sorry. I think I'm more tired than I realized. I am truly sorry for your loss."

"It's not the only thing I miss," Carnelian continued. "I was quite the ladies' man, and this body—"

"Carnelian!" Lazuli interrupted. "That is not the type of thing we discuss in proper company!"

He chose to pout instead of reply.

Bevin redirected the conversation. "What about you Lazuli? What did you do?"

"Ah, I was one of the lucky ones. Mum to three littles. My husband was a blacksmith and we lived a quiet life. I never expected to become a golem." Lazuli's face turned down with sadness.

"I'm sorry. You must miss them a great deal."

"It gets better with time, and I've certainly had plenty of that. They passed away before I became a golem, anyway. A sickness killed nearly half of the dwarves under our mountain at the time. I helped figure out the cure, but they were already gone. It did result in me being offered this opportunity, though."

"So you're a healer?"

"I am. I was tempted to live out the rest of my life and return to my family, but I knew that I could do more good this way. Someday I will return to them—when it's time."

Venlian spoke for the first time since Adalyn had sat next to him. "That's very noble of you."

"Thank you." Lazuli looked away, lost in the memories of her past.

Iolite cleared his throat. "I guess it's my turn. As they said, I am an original. I didn't do any noble and great thing as the others have. I was just a volunteer. I never really found my calling while I was a dwarf still and saw an ad. I had nothing to lose—literally."

Nolan held up a hand. "Wait a minute. You were a volunteer, and ended up being in charge of these guys?"

"I am quite a bit older them. As more and more golems were made, I ended up guiding many of them. Helped them adjust. I was never officially put into a leadership position."

"It's true," Carnelian added. "When I joined, there weren't any sort of rankings. The golems started to form their own groups around the time I became one. Some disappeared and found their own homes, a group retreated deep into one of the sacred mountains and became monks of sorts, others picked fights and hired themselves out as mercenaries. Iolite was sort of a middle ground."

Images of golems in robes chanting in candlelight flashed through Adalyn's mind, and she snorted. Everyone turned to look at her.

"I'm sorry. That's not funny. I just… I'm just tired. So Iolite was a volunteer, Lazuli a healer, Carnelian a bard. Merit, I know you were a prince, but why did you become a golem?"

"It was a trade," Carnelian said before Merit had a chance. It was clear he was used to dominating conversation.

"Yes, it was a trade," Merit said, shooting him a look. "I was entrusted with building several expansions onto a castle. This castle, actually, and I needed laborers who weren't afraid of being out from under the mountain and who wouldn't be easily injured. I struck a deal."

Adalyn toyed with the end of her braid. "They let you become a golem in exchange for them helping you? That doesn't make sense. You are the only one who benefits from that."

"Not exactly. We wanted him more than his own people did," Carnelian cut in again.

"Will you stop that?" Merit snapped before turning back to Adalyn. "They hadn't been in contact with the dwarven group who made golems for several hundred years. Several groups have become stronger than others and started attacking other groups of golems. Iolite wanted to increase his numbers a bit."

"I've heard of battle fields where these attacks have happened," Bevin said. "Traders enter the mountains where golem groups have retreated only to find piles of crumbled rocks."

Adalyn gasped. "I completely forgot that in Chors this is all happening now! How are they killing golems?"

All of her rocky friends shook their heads.

"We don't know," Lazuli answered.

The room sat in silence as everything sunk in. Adalyn tried but couldn't stifle a yawn.

"I'm so sorry. I think I need a nap. Let's talk about what happened when I returned to Pieriun last night so I can get some rest."

CHAPTER TEN

The rumble from her stomach told Adalyn that she had slept longer than she'd intended. She needed to return to Pieriun, but decided to grab a snack first to recharge before completely draining herself worldwalking through the living spell again.

She started for the door to see if the guards were there and stopped short. Why was she doing that? She didn't need to. An image of the kitchen formed in her mind, and in an instant she was there.

"I wondered when I would see you again."

Adalyn spun around towards the voice. "Oh! It's you. You scared me!"

Neith sat at the same spot at the table as the last time Adalyn had ventured here.

"Have any more of that cake?" Adalyn asked.

"This one is even better. There's mint in the chocolate frosting. A dollop of sweetened whipped cream, and it's the most heavenly thing you've ever had."

Her mouth watering already, Adalyn quickly joined

Neith and took the slice that had just been placed on the plate. She was relieved to find that this cake didn't seem to be faulty like the last one had been. It stayed moist all the way down.

She let out a small moan of pleasure. "How have I never had anything quite like this?"

"Your kingdom has had no magic, or at least no open magic use in it, correct?"

Adalyn nodded as she took another bite.

"Something like this would be difficult to keep. Our cook's ability helps keep things cool no matter the weather. It also helps that she is, in fact, a woman."

"I thought that Chors didn't let women do job… type… things. Sorry, this cake is very distracting."

Neith chuckled. "After our last one died, they put out a call for potential cooks to apply from all over our kingdom. They usually promote from within, but we've had several schools to teach this sort of thing pop up over the years. She dressed as a man, and it wasn't until after she had worked here for several months that her gender was discovered. By that time, Queen Faith wouldn't let her go. Would you like another?"

Scooting her plate forward was all the reply Neith needed.

"What do you do here?"

"You mean besides eat cake? I'm a friend of the family. I help where I can."

Choosing not to pry into the woman's occupation when prying clearly wasn't wanted, Adalyn decided to use this opportunity to ask simpler questions instead.

"Do you have a husband?"

"Of a sort. He's really a good man, but we will see. How about you? Is there someone in your life?"

"I'm only seventeen."

"That's not a no."

Adalyn set her fork on her plate and took a deep breath. "There's been someone, but I don't really know what's happening there. Then there's someone else that has me very confused. I don't think I'm in a relationship."

"My dear, it sounds like you may need to sit down and have a serious conversation."

"Isn't that the truth." Adalyn stood up and rinsed her plate and fork and set it back on the table. "I'm amazed by so much here. How does Chors have water that runs into the buildings like a small waterfall?"

"Magic. Remember, we never lost ours. Pieriun once had this, as well."

"You can't be serious!"

Neith shook her head with a smile. "I swear it's true. The last time I was there, most homes had it."

"I feel like so much was lost."

"It can be returned."

"I would love to see that." Adalyn hopped up from her seat. "I should be getting back before anyone misses me. Thank you for everything."

"Of course. I hope we meet again. Perhaps tomorrow night there may be another flavor of cake that you can try."

Adalyn smiled. "I can only hope."

She closed her eyes and took a deep breath, preparing herself for the jump. She wasn't going back to the guest suite but was heading straight to Pieriun. When she opened her eyes, a wave of exhaustion hit her, and she sat down on her bed. Back in her pitch-black room in the tunnels, she decided that sleep would be the best option for now. No one wanted whatever the consequences would be of her dealing with things when she was this worn out. Tucking herself in, she closed her eyes and allowed sleep to take her.

When she awoke, she felt as if she had aged a decade or more—stiff all over and as if she had gotten into the wine stores.

"You're awake." Glenda's voice startled Adalyn.

Her hand to her heart, Adalyn sat up. "Why do people keep doing that to me?"

"Excuse me?"

Pulling the blankets back and kicking her feet over the edge of the bed, she replied, "Never mind. How did you know I was here?"

"I felt you. I may not be able to use my ability as I am, but it's still a part of me, and it called to you when you returned, just as it felt as if a part of me was ripped away when you left."

"What? That sounds terrible!"

Glenda watched as Adalyn dressed in a fresh uniform. "Our abilities are usually only called to one person at a time. Others may have similar ones, but no two are exactly the same. It seems that we are connected. Others have felt it as well. Many of the spirits have left here because of the call of their ability in others."

"Is that why there have been very few people with magic since the Great War? Part of the ability was trapped in the living spell, so it couldn't manifest itself?"

"It could be. We will never know. You should hurry, though. There's been a message that one of the towns in the mountains has had a strange illness strike it and attacks happening near it."

"How can I help with that? I'm not a healer."

Glenda just stared at her.

"What?"

"Can you think of a quick way to get them there and potentially save more lives?"

Adalyn realized what Glenda meant. "You know my ability doesn't work like that. I have to know where I'm going."

"You know Greshmier very well."

She shook her head. "Not there."

"You're their best bet."

The last thing Adalyn expected was to be heading back to her hometown. She hadn't returned after the money ran out and she'd had to leave school. There was nothing left for her there, and the memories were too painful.

"All right," she sighed. "Let's go."

She opened her door to find the hall filled with Banneret dressed in their blues, carrying large sacks and hollering out requests for items up and down the dorm. It was slightly unsettling, yet exciting. Every other time she had been down here it had been empty, and it now felt as if the life was being breathed back into it.

"Greshmier is waiting! Have your horses saddled and ready to go in thirty minutes!" a familiar voice called through the crowd.

"Eridu?" Adalyn shifted, trying to find her friend among all the others.

"Captain Adalyn?" Eridu replied.

The hallway went suddenly silent. Eridu's progress in her direction could be seen by the parting of people until she stood in front of Adalyn.

"You're here! I'm so glad to see you!" Eridu greeted with a glowing smile.

"You, too. I heard you're going to Greshmier?"

Eridu gestured to the people filling the hall. "They are. I have a list of things in the office we need to go over for placements and changes that I need your approval for. If you want to wait for me there, we can discuss those when I'm done here."

"Actually, we will need to wait on that for a bit."

"Did you need to do something first?"

"I'm going with them. I can get them there much faster."

"Do you know where Greshmier is?"

Adalyn smiled. "In fact, I do. I should let the King know I'm here before we head out. Do you mind putting together supplies for me? I can make this a short trip for everyone, but I don't know where any of the supplies are anymore."

"Of course!" Eridu noticed that the Banneret were still watching. "Twenty-eight minutes left! I hope you're ready. It looks like your captain is coming with you!"

Adalyn couldn't help but smile watching her friend. It seemed that much had changed over the several weeks she had been in Chors.

Adalyn looked over the group. It seemed that a small army had been gathered for this trip. King Coeus hadn't been too happy that she was leaving immediately after returning, but he agreed that her ability to make a several-week trip much shorter benefited not only his people, but would benefit him, as well. She could pop back for updates and return if things went south.

"It's an impressive group, isn't it?" Brinn said as he approached from behind.

"It really is. I almost feel like a fraud being in charge of so many people. I'm never around, and nearly half of those coming with us are Banneret."

"Those of us who came from Chors understand how important your mission there is better than anyone else could. It's worth it."

She only nodded and watched as the soldiers and Banneret were organized into groups. She would transport fifty at a time, all while saddled up on horses in case they needed them over there.

"I'm going to scout ahead. I need to find somewhere that will be safe to transport everyone to without stirring up too much trouble."

Before Brinn could object, she pictured a small glade just outside the town and jumped. She was immediately drenched by pummeling rain. Pulling the hood of her cloak up over her head, she darted towards the trees and turned to look around. The space seemed empty, and the rain would deter people from stumbling on them as she brought everyone here.

With a deep breath, she jumped back next to Brinn.

Water flung off her cloak as she shook it off, splattering those around her.

"Hey!" a nearby soldier complained.

"Put on your cloak and any other rain gear you have. It's pouring there. Prep yourself and your horse. Spread the word."

She watched as the man went to relay her message.

"How did he know to actually listen to me?"

"Do you forget that your uniform says your rank? What did you think that silver moon means?"

"Truly? I have no idea what any of this stuff on my uniform means."

Brinn chuckled. "Sometimes I forget that you didn't become captain the way Glenda did."

"Are those who worldwalk usually the captain?"

"The position goes to whoever is right for the job. I don't think there's ever been two with the same ability in a row before."

She nodded in thought. "So you knew Glenda?"

"She was a brilliant chess player, though a bit of a cheat."

Adalyn glanced around to see if her spirit friend was nearby, but she was nowhere to be seen. "Some time you're going to have to tell me about her."

"I would love to."

CHAPTER ELEVEN

Adalyn spent the better part of an hour transporting everyone. The glade was far enough away from the town that it couldn't be seen, but she could still see the path she had worn as a child between the two. Miraculously, Adalyn wasn't exhausted. It seemed her efforts traveling through the living spell had done much to strengthen her ability.

Tents filled the glade, and horses were tied to nearly every tree in sight. The ability to keep their goods dry was everyone's first priority. Brinn and the other leaders were busy giving orders for setting up camp. Unsure where to go, Adalyn felt a familiar pull towards town and decided to follow it. From experience she knew that if she didn't listen to it, it would only get stronger.

The ten-minute walk took nearly thirty as she rerouted around the swollen creek and slid on the slick mud and grass.

Memories of herself as a small child crept into her mind as the town came into view. Being chased through the forest paths. Sharing a slice of apple pie at the fall festival, and the procession of her parents returning from merchant trips were so vivid in her mind that she could almost see them before her eyes.

The townspeople were in their homes due to the heavy rain, and Adalyn darted from porch to porch and ducked under cover of any ledge she could find. The pull became stronger as she moved through the town until she stood in front of her own home far on the other side. While the others had light peeking through the cracks on the shutters and the smell of fire smoke poured from their chimneys, her old home sat dark and still.

The door groaned as she entered, and every step made the floor creak. The house had been gutted. She could easily move through the dark space without a light because everything was gone.

As she moved through the house, continuing to follow the pull, she brushed her fingers along the walls. How long had it sat empty? A seam next to the stairs cut her finger. She sucked on the small wound while investigating further. No other wall had a mark like this.

An urgency from her ability encouraged her to gently push on the wall, and a soft click followed by another groan told her that this seam wasn't from the home being in disrepair.

Adalyn opened the small hidden door and found a stash of papers, coins, and other valuables.

"I always find you in the most interesting of places," Glenda said.

"I don't know if you can call this interesting," Adalyn replied as she pulled the stash out of the wall and set it on the floor, willing her heart to calm after the start Glenda's arrival had given it.

"There're several broken boards upstairs, and the chimney is in decent enough shape. You should start a fire and dry off before you get sick."

"How do you know the chimney is safe?"

Glenda gave her a look. "I'm a spirit. One of the benefits is that I can walk through walls, remember? A regular inspection of the chimneys from the dorms and common room was also part of my job when I was captain. Can you imagine what would happen if a fire happened while we were trapped underground? When you are back more steadily, it will become part of your role, as well. Our ability makes us the perfect people for it."

A chill went down Adalyn's spine as she imagined having to sit inside a wall from the dorms deep underground all the way up, inspecting the chimneys. She'd never cared for tight spaces.

Adalyn stood up and left to gather the wood. When she returned, she found Glenda staring at the papers she'd found.

"Before you start that, would you mind spreading these out a little? I would like to take a look."

Setting the pile of wood next to the fireplace, Adalyn spread out the items she had removed from the wall and returned to get the fire going.

"It appears these are your parents' manifests, log sheets, and plans for expansion. When did you last see them?"

Kneeling, Adalyn struck her flint and steel over the wood. It quickly caught, and she rejoined her friend.

"I was sent to a boarding school when I was eight. They visited occasionally as they passed by for business. I last saw them just before my thirteenth birthday. They were heading to the port and were lost at sea."

"I'm sorry to hear that. There may be pages missing, but it looks like they were heading to the other side of Chors. I wonder..."

Adalyn waited for Glenda to continue. "Yes?"

"You know how we've talked about how all of Chors was trapped in the spell?"

"Yes."

"Well, it's not the only kingdom on that continent. Another one had gone silent not too long before the Great War started. Twisted beings, such as the death slaugh that you ran into before we officially met, started to emerge from Almendra in overwhelming numbers. What if the living spell wasn't just on Chors? What if it was on the entire continent, and possibly even covered part of the sea?" A gust of wind made the fire flicker, and Adalyn glanced between it and Glenda.

The name of the kingdom sounded familiar, but she couldn't quite place it. "Are you telling me that their ship was sunk by something magical?"

"I'm not sure, but I may know someone who can help. I have to go. I'll return as soon as I can." Glenda touched Adalyn's arm, and a moment later, she was gone.

Adalyn sat by the fire and stared into the flames. The fire was warm and comforting, but she knew that tomorrow would be busy. If she wanted to get through these papers anytime soon, now was the best time to do it. She spread some of the papers and laid down on her stomach to read them. Eventually she'd have to return to camp for some much-needed rest, and when she woke, she had lots of work to do.

The morning light woke Adalyn, and she groaned as she realized she'd fallen asleep on the hard wooden floor. She stretched and grabbed the papers she'd unwittingly abandoned nearby. A quick glance last night had told her the pages weren't in any type of order. The last one she remembered looking at had been a ledger, and since it had put her to sleep, she set it aside. Adalyn flipped through the other papers until she found a letter addressed to the late Queen Elizabeth. Reading the first few sentences, Adalyn checked the date and realized she was reading one of her parents' last letters before they disappeared.

The letter concerned several of their ships. A large group of them had gone out to sea and had yet to return. Maybe Glenda was right. Maybe they had been trapped in the living spell.

Adalyn rose and dusted herself off. As much as she wanted answers, she had other priorities right now. She needed to be in the streets, helping the Banneret and organizing their aid. The townspeople all had to be in the process of grieving their sick and dead, but eventually life would move on.

The walk through the town was both heartbreaking and joyous for Adalyn. She hadn't been back since she was a little girl, but so much of it was the same. A few familiar faces, aged a number of years just as hers had, appeared in the crowd gathering around the king's men she had transported here. Would anyone recognize her?

Looking over the crowd, it appeared that everything was in hand. A sort of organized chaos was in process to ensure that those inflicted with the illness were being treated. The way that many of the Banneret who had come with her could help heal these people made Adalyn almost feel as if her own ability was a bit less wonderful—not because she couldn't help others with it, but because so far everything she had done helped indirectly, never solving problems on her own.

Her stomach grumbled as the wind carried the smell of bread her way. She could almost feel the crunch of the crust in her mouth already. Deciding to grab a bite on her way to finding Brinn, she followed the smell towards the bakery. Her body moved almost as if by memory.

A small crowd of women gathered within the shop and peered out the windows. Adalyn worked her way past them to the counter. She eyed a loaf of sourdough on display. A memory of coming in this same shop with her parents flashed in her mind. She'd ridden on her father's shoulders while her mother paid for a loaf of sourdough before they headed into the forest for a picnic.

Sourdough it is, she thought.

She purchased the bread and began working her way outside, taking the time to rip of a chunk and savor a bite as she did so.

"I wonder if they were there last night?"

"Where?"

"In the old Mernt home."

Adalyn's feet slowed as she strove to listen.

"Who's foolish enough to go in there? Doesn't everyone know that place is cursed?"

What could these women be talking about? Adalyn's home had never been cursed. It had been beautiful and elegant.

"Of course they don't know that, Misty. They came from the capital."

"But how did they get here? No one saw them coming through."

"Maybe they aren't afraid of the curse because they deal with the dark arts, as well. I mean, look at them."

Adalyn followed their line of sight and saw them warily eyeing her Banneret. She cleared her throat. "Can I ask how the Mernt home became cursed?"

Only a few of the women turned to look at her, and when they saw she was an outsider, immediately returned their gaze to outside. A plump older woman with a mess of blonde hair slowly turned her head back and gave Adalyn a look-over.

"You know, you kind of look like them."

"Who?"

"The Mernts. And now that I think of it, like one of them," the woman nodded her head back outside without breaking eye contact.

"You mean the Banneret? The ones in blue?" Adalyn gestured to her uniform with the loaf of bread, leaving crumbs all over herself.

The woman's eyes grew wide. "Banneret? So it is magic."

Adalyn couldn't keep the slight smile from forming on her face. "They're just here to help."

Another of the women turned to face Adalyn. "Still don't mean we have to trust it. You know, Gladys, you're right. She sort of does look like a Mernt."

Adalyn's grin grew larger.

Gladys elbowed another woman to get her to turn around and pointed at Adalyn. "Don't you think she looks sorta like Kathrine, but with Jin's eyes?"

Adalyn took another bite of her bread while they eyed her. "Maybe that's because I am," she replied, crumbs flying out of her mouth.

Gladys's loud gasp caused the rest of the women to turn around quickly. "No, you can't be. She's been gone for… Oh gosh, by now she would be about your—"

Shouts and screams drowned out the rest of her sentence, and Adalyn ran to the doorway and drew her sword. Her stomach dropped when she saw what had caused such a commotion.

A group of monsters hacked their way through the crowd, spreading chaos as they went. Death slaughs and a variety of monsters that she had only seen once before—in that last book she had read back in Chors—tore into people and tossed them aside. She didn't know if the soldiers who weren't Banneret had weapons that could do anything against them. Much as she didn't want to, she had to do something.

Calling upon her ability, she appeared behind a tall, hairy beast with droopy ears and a gut and slashed across its spine. Before it collapsed, she had already jumped behind the next creature and repeated the process, continuing to do so again and again. Sometimes she had to add a slice to the gut or throat if they didn't collapse immediately.

Her head began to ache from the heavy use of her ability, but she knew she had to push through. After fighting through what felt like an eternity, she stood in the middle of a pile of slain beasts, blood splattering her face and soaking her clothes.

She looked at the twitching beasts around her, the world around her muted. Something grabbed her arm, and she turned with her sword ready.

Brinn jumped back, both arms raised. "It's just me. You okay?"

"I'm sorry. I," she shook her head to force herself to focus, "I'm all right." Taking note of the blood covering her fellow Banneret, she added, "Are you all right?"

He nodded. "I'm fine. All of the Banneret are safe, and only a few injuries among the soldiers. We are still taking a count, but there were several of the townspeople killed in the attack." Brinn ran a shaking hand through his hair, causing it to stick straight up and smearing blood on his forehead.

"How much battle did you see in Chors?"

"Some. It wasn't like this, though. The people themselves were spared when we passed through. Only soldiers were attacked. This… this was a slaughter. You, though. If it wasn't for you, this would have been much worse. You understated your skill."

Adalyn remembered the church in Chors and the story that she had been told there. It appeared not all of the

Pieriun troops had held to the honor code of not attacking the people.

"My actual sword skills are lacking. I'm working on improving them. If it wasn't for my ability, I wouldn't have been nearly as much help."

"That's the way of the Banneret, though. You adapt your fighting style to fit your ability."

Brinn left her to aid a healer. Adalyn looked around and saw that the Banneret were already helping the injured and set herself to work to assist. What all she could do, she didn't know, but she refused to just watch when she had two good working hands.

CHAPTER TWELVE

The cold of the creek helped Adalyn's mind clear as she cleaned blood off herself. After the mess in town was taken care of, Brinn had pulled her aside and questioned her whereabouts.

"Where did you go?" he'd asked. "You just…disappeared, without so much as a word. We didn't know what to think last night."

A long discussion later, she'd explained more about herself than she'd felt comfortable with and had promised Brinn she wouldn't disappear without notice.

After that, she was finally able to go clean up. She sighed, grateful to have a moment away from the others so she could have a few minutes alone to process what had happened.

Adalyn froze as a twig snapped behind her. Her hand on her hilt, she whirled around to find an odd blue man with reptilian skin and a wide slit for a mouth staring at her wide-eyed.

"Who are you?" she asked.

He slowly raised his hands a little and a pink forked tongue darted out of his mouth before he spoke.

"Was I brought to you? We don't have this kind of forest, so that must be what happened." His head cocked to one side. "Do you want to come see?"

Adalyn looked around to make sure that she was, in fact, the only person there.

"Are you talking to me?"

The blue man only cocked his head to the other side and looked at her with a blank expression. "Do you not need us?"

"I'm beyond confused right now. Do you need help? Can I take you somewhere?"

He turned around and retreated into the forest. "Maybe they got it wrong," he mumbled. "They don't usually get it wrong, but there's always going to be a first. Perhaps that Banneret's spell is beginning to fade."

Adalyn chased after him. "Excuse me! Did you just say Banneret?"

He stopped so suddenly she bumped into him.

"Yes. The Banneret who cast the spell to protect the forge. We are the caretakers and specialists."

The forge! Glenda had been so mysterious about anything regarding the forge. Even after digging through all the books she could find, Adalyn never found any mention of it.

"Perhaps you are looking for me. I am a Banneret."

He scoffed. "Obviously. Just look at you in your uniform with all those shiny buttons. How someone who is leading the Banneret hasn't had the forge call them already is beyond me. Of course, it has been a long time since we saw one of you. Perhaps that's why."

She watched his fidgeting fingers as he sputtered out the not-nonsense nonsense, trying to decide if this possibly insane man was truly safe to depart with.

"I have been waiting. Do I need to do anything or come back later?"

He shook his head very quickly. "No. No, you don't want to do that. We won't be here later, and then it will be too late. You can follow me if you want to go to the forge. Or not. It's your choice."

"Absolutely! I want to go."

"First, a test. You must answer this riddle to prove worthy."

It seemed rather odd that she was supposed to go to this forge but needed to do a test first, but she had waited for a long time.

"All right, what's the riddle?"

"What color are blueberries?"

Adalyn thought for a moment. This had to be a trick, right? There's no way that this could be so easy.

"Blue."

"Nope! They are red."

Her jaw dropped. "What? No, they're not. They're as blue as you are!"

The man's hands quickly patted over his body as his eyes bounced over each spot they landed. "What? I'm blue?"

"You didn't know?"

"Of course, I knew. I just always thought I was red.

Maybe your blue is my red. Who gets to decide these things?"

"Why do you think blueberries are called blueberries?"

He thought for a moment. "Perhaps you're right. I will need to think on this." He turned and began to walk away again. "Are you coming? I'm Roust, by the way."

Adalyn did a quick check that she had grabbed all of her belongings and followed after him. *So much for not disappearing without notice*, she thought. She winced as she thought about all the people expecting her in different places and mentally apologized to Brinn. Hopefully going to the forge wouldn't take too long.

"You're what?"

"My name. It's Roust."

"Oh. I'm Adalyn."

"It's very nice to meet you, Adalyn. Keep up. The way will not stay open much longer."

She made sure to stay as close to the blue reptilian man as possible without stepping on his heels. The brush around them grew thick the further they went, and thorns began to catch her clothing. She focused on watching his legs seamlessly work through the plants as she tried to follow the same path that seemingly only he knew.

After a few minutes of pure focus, the sound of voices caught her attention, and when she looked up, she realized that he had been right. Where she had been in a forest of mostly pines, she was now surrounded by leafy trees, and it felt slightly warmer than before. She hadn't noticed crossing through a barrier of any sort, but she definitely wasn't where she had been before.

She continued to follow him into a small village of

stone houses with slate roofs. No building seemed to be built from any sort of timber—rather odd, she thought, considering they were surrounded by trees.

She gaped at tiny dragons playing in the fields and streets. A large blue dragon flew above her with three small ones in tow. Adalyn watched as it landed gracefully in the field to her right. The three small dragons attempted to follow suit, but failed in the most adorable way. One face-planted into the ground. Another rolled after putting one foot on the ground too soon, and the last almost made it, but a gust of wind caught its wings, and it landed on its rear. After a quick inspection, they all took off again.

A glint of gold on the large blue dragon caught her eye, and looking closer, she noted that quite a few of the dragon's scales glinted gold, silver, and a rainbow of colors.

"That's incredible."

"What is?"

"The scales on that dragon. It's not entirely blue."

He continued walking without turning to look. "That's their hoard."

Adalyn nearly tripped over her own feet while craning her neck to keep looking at the magnificent beast.

"In stories, dragons hold their hoard in caves. Are dragons actually born that way?"

Roust broke out in laughter. "You silly humans. Are we born with our hoards? Classic."

"I was only asking."

He imitated her voice in a squeaky high pitch. "*I was only asking*. Having a hoard literally means to gather it and protect it from others. It's your property that no one else can touch. Of course, since we can't get out anymore, ours are either passed down, traded, or won in one-on-one combat."

They entered a tavern. It was fairly small, but considering that they apparently had little to no communication with the outside world, and therefore no travelers, it made sense. She followed him to a table just in view of the kitchen. More small dragons ran around, assisting a reptilian woman with soft horns while she cooked.

"Roust, how does the treasure get onto the dragon?"

He shivered. "Only the strongest have hoards. Not only do you usually have to earn it, but you pull your scales out and replace them with each piece."

Her jaw dropped as her stomach turned at the thought. "That's gruesome."

"Yep! It's why I don't have any. Nope, not for me. Besides, I'm handsome as I am. Don't you think so?"

She gave him a slight smile, unsure what exactly to say.

The woman from the kitchen wiped her hands on her apron and approached the pair. "I see we have a visitor! First one in several generations. Welcome to Makylite."

"Thank you. I'm glad to be here."

"Have you traveled far? Are you hungry?"

After being interrupted from breakfast by the attack and the constant use of her ability, she was starving.

"I would love something."

The woman put a hand on her hip, a warm smile on her face. "Dinner won't be ready for a few, but we do have créme brû

léé chilling for dessert."

Having no idea what that was, Adalyn looked to Roust for guidance, only to finding him nodding his head very enthusiastically.

"May I have one, too?" he asked, practically bouncing in his chair.

The woman rolled her eyes. "Of course. We will prepare them and bring them right out."

Adalyn watched as one of the small dragons shifted to a young reptilian girl and pulled two small bowls out of a box, setting them on the counter. A mist rose from the box when the lid was opened.

She turned to Roust, eyes wide as realization hit her. "You're a dragon? Why didn't you tell me?"

He only shrugged. "I sort of did. You just didn't listen."

Turning back to the kitchen, she saw the girl sprinkle sugar onto the bowls and then beckon a very tiny dragon over. She lifted the dragon up to the bowls, and it blew a small flame over the top. After a quick snuggle, the girl set the tiny dragon down and brought the bowls over with a pair of small spoons. With a shy smile, she hurried back into the kitchen.

Picking up the spoon, Adalyn cracked the golden caramelized sugar layer and scooped a small bite of cream-colored pudding with some of the sugar and brought it to her nose. The smell of vanilla and the recently broiled sugar made her mouth water. As soon as it hit her tongue, a small moan escaped her, and her eyes closed as she savored it.

"This is amazing!"

Her eyes opened to see that Roust was licking his bowl

clean. He stopped when he realized she was watching him and gently put the bowl down on the table. "I'm sorry. It's just so good."

She could only laugh as she dug into her next bite, mentally taking note that she had to get the recipe before she left.

Licking the spoon after her last bite, a thought hit her. "Roust, is there any way to contact anyone outside of here? Can I go back with my ability and come back, or can you get a message out? They've got to be worried back home, and technically I'm part of the command, even though I don't really know what all that entails yet."

"Sorry, but if you leave, you won't be able to come back until the forge decides you are ready again. We have no communication with the outside world. That was part of the bargain when the spell was put up to protect us and the forge."

After a day of exploring and mingling with the friendly Makylites, Adalyn was so grateful for a bed at the tavern and fell asleep almost as soon as her head the pillow.

The spirit of an extremely large blue dragon nudged her in her sleep, encouraging her to follow it. She didn't understand why it didn't speak, but chose to take its lead.

They flew through the village, but it wasn't the village she'd been in. It was much larger, and there were many more Makylites, yet it was in the same location. The dragon soared around the village and looked towards the nearby lake.

At first she didn't see anything. As she continued to watch, though, something large glistened in the sun as it moved towards the village. The closer it got, the muddier it looked, and Adalyn realized that it was water. Somehow the lake was flooding, and it was coming straight for the village.

The dragon cried out, but no one could hear it. Adalyn also cried out, even though she knew it was fruitless. She closed her eyes as the wall of water hit the village, but even her hands over her ears couldn't block out the cries that turned to silence below her. She didn't know if it was because it was really that loud or if it was some side effect from worldwalking to see this.

The dragon nudged her spirit and they moved towards the lake. There she saw many massive logs and stones chaotically dispersed around the area.

Dam, a voice said in her mind.

Adalyn found the dragon looking at her expectantly and assumed the voice must have been from them. Her parents had talked of dams on their travels. They were used to help create irrigation systems to grow better crops in larger areas. She had never seen one, though.

The dragon looked back at the village and let out a heartbroken cry. Adalyn didn't know what exactly its connection with the inhabitants had been, but since its spirit was somehow guiding hers to this vision of what she assumed was the past, she could feel how deeply it felt this loss.

Adalyn floated closer and put her hand on its neck, the

only thing she could think to do to try and comfort it. It nuzzled her, and she felt her spirit released from it with a faint echo of thanks.

Her spirit returned to her time and body, and the rest of the night she slept a deep, dreamless sleep.

CHAPTER THIRTEEN

After a hearty breakfast the next morning, Roust appeared in the tavern practically bouncing up and down.

"You're in for a treat today! We've decided to honor you by inviting you to see one of our tournaments."

Adalyn set her plate on the counter and turned to face him. "What kind of tournament?"

Roust's grin was like that of a small child with a wonderful secret. "Uh-uh. I'm not going to tell you. You have to come see."

She followed him out of the tavern to the edge of town to find a row of targets lined up. The entire village had turned out with bows and arrows.

"You're archers? Why do dragons need to know how to do archery?"

"We are the specialists for the Banneret archery forge. It's part of the trade. We are protected in the barrier from being hunted, and in return, use our ability to make unbreakable bows and arrows."

He handed her his bow and a single arrow. It vibrated in her hand as she ran her hand down the bow and plucked the string. The arrow was perfectly straight, with blue feathers she had never seen on any bird.

"What's so special about these? Why are you the specialists?"

"The forge experience is… unique. It's not something I can explain, but when our scales are used as part of the process, they create the sharpest, most dangerous bows and arrows in the world. Makylites are connected to the earth. We help things grow, but we don't handle the cold very well. It's why we stay near the DJ and their sword forge. They are fire attuned and keep the area warm year-round."

"What happens when you get cold?"

He leaned in and whispered, "We freeze. Literally can't move. Originally, in our old home before we came here, we lived in large forests and in the trees. Occasionally we would fall out of the trees." He pulled back and shrugged. "Couldn't move to catch ourselves."

Adalyn leaned into him and whispered back, "Why are you whispering? I'm the only one here who didn't know this."

"Oh yeah!" Roust broke out in a laugh.

"So, who are the DJ?"

"They're another group of dragons, like the ones here. They specialize in forging blades, just as we are experts at creating weapons for archers."

Adalyn watched as the Makylites began to line up in front of the targets. One after another, they shot and somehow missed every single target. Round after round, every single arrow missed the mark. A few of them hit someone else's target, and those were much celebrated.

"Aren't they supposed to actually hit the target? I thought that you guys were good at archery," she asked.

Roust didn't look her way, his focus on the next round of archers as they lined up. "That's what makes us so dangerous. The unpredictability is part of that."

Brow raised, she watched as this group followed the pattern of the last. None of them hit their own targets, either. "If you say so."

Roust held out his hand to take back his bow and arrow. "All right, it's my turn!"

"Good luck!"

He waved her off. "Thanks, but I don't need it. I'm the best we have."

She highly doubted that he didn't need luck, based on what she had seen so far. After the next group gathered and claimed their targets, the first volley was sent, and no arrows hit their mark. The cheering from the crowd only bolstered the confidence of those competing.

The second round followed the same pattern yet again. Adalyn let out a cheer as Roust raised for his final shot and hit the very edge of his target.

He ran around in excitement, bow still in hand. The crowd swarmed him with congratulations. Once they departed, he rejoined Adalyn.

"You did it!"

"Of course I did. I told you I was the best." He held up a large piece of gold in the shape of a scale. "I'm not sure what I'm going to do with this, though. I'm not interested in a hoard. Do you want it?"

Adalyn held up her hands and took a step back. "I can't! It's yours. You just won that!"

He gestured up and down his body. "I have everything I need. Truly, I would just give it to someone else if I didn't give it to you."

"Are you sure? We just met."

He shoved the golden scale in her hands. "Will you just take it already?"

"You're rather odd for a dragon, aren't you?"

He looked at her. "You know many well to compare me to?"

She shook her head. "No, but it's obvious that you're even different from the ones here."

"That's true. It's because I'm the gatekeeper for our forge. You aren't so normal, either. My connection with the spell sometimes makes me a bit...odd."

"How so?"

"The forge calls the Banneret only to the forge they need to go to. You need the sword forge with the DJ, yet I was the gatekeeper called to let you in."

"I didn't know that. How do I get to the correct forge, then?"

He shook his head again. "You wouldn't have met us if you didn't need us, too. I just don't know why. If you would like, I can bring you to the sword forge tomorrow. Maybe we can find something there. I do warn you, though, they can be a bit unruly. We don't exactly get along."

"That would be wonderful, thank you."

She watched as the village of dragons celebrated around her. Families with many small dragons and children running around were everywhere.

"Roust? Is it normal for a dragon to have a large family?"

"No. Why?"

"There are just a lot of young here."

A darkness crossed his face. "A long time ago, there was a flood. It wiped out most of our adults. We live very long lifespans, and most of the young you see were still in eggs when it hit. The few adults, including myself, were in the mountain when it hit. These are mostly orphans."

The dragon and dream from the night before came to Adalyn's mind. Perhaps she was called here for a reason after all.

The DJs lived much closer to the Makylites than Adalyn had anticipated. It was only a short walk before she was already in their village. It looked similar to the one she had just come from: all stone buildings, with a mix of red dragons and lizard-like people running about.

Afraid to enter the village himself, Roust had left her on the outskirts and wished her good luck before retreating, muttering to himself about disorganized beasts.

An exceptionally tall DJ stepped in front of her. "How did you get here?"

"I w-w-was escorted here." Adalyn stumbled over her words, startled.

The woman rolled her eyes. "I saw *that.* I meant, how did you get through the barrier? I see that you're a Banneret, but I didn't escort anyone in."

"Oh! Roust let me in."

"That no good, uptight... trying to pass off his work onto me." The dragon woman grabbed Adalyn's shoulders and turned her about. "Go back to him and tell him that I'm not sending you back."

Adalyn brushed the woman's hands from her body and stood her ground. "No, I'm supposed to be here." She drew her sword and presented it in front of her.

The woman looked at it. "How odd." She turned on her heel and walked several steps. "Are you coming?" she called without looking back.

From the way she talked, Adalyn assumed the woman was the keeper for the DJ and that this spell the Banneret had put in place may affect the one connected to it more than they realized. She quickly followed so as not to be left behind.

To her surprise, they walked through the village and began climbing higher in the mountain. No words were spoken, just the two of them and the creatures scurrying around.

A break in the trees opened up the view of a valley. The Makylite village was below in the deepest part of the valley, a rebuilt dam creating a shimmering lake near it. The DJ village was tucked into the side of one of the mountains, inside a perfect bowl carved out of stone.

Adalyn only paused for a moment to look so she wouldn't lose her guide. After a long hike, the entrance to a cave appeared. Without stopping, they entered. The small entrance opened into a massive cavern. The glow of hot coals gave light to the empty space.

"Hmm. He isn't here."

"Who isn't here?"

"The forge master. You will have to wait or come back later. I can stay with you for a while, if you wish."

The way that the woman kept glancing at the entrance told Adalyn that she clearly did not want to stay here.

Adalyn gave her a reassuring smile. "I'm fine. I can wait."

Relief apparent on her face, the woman took a few steps towards the exit. "If you wish. If he takes too long to show up, feel free to return. My name is Trisht. Just ask for me at the tavern and they will send someone to come find me."

"Thank you."

The woman left with a small nod, and Adalyn was left to her own thoughts.

At first she wandered around the forge itself, investigating the various tools and exploring the space. She had no idea how to forge anything, and the task ahead of her was daunting. When she found a small cave off of the main one, she peeked in to find a bed and shelves filled with various jars and boxes. Assuming that must be the forge master's living quarters, she left it alone.

Bored, she stepped outside the cavern and back onto the mountain side. The trees were too thick to see much. Afraid she would get lost if she ventured into them, she chose to return to the cavern and wait a bit longer before heading down the mountain.

After finding a comfortable spot to rest, her conversation with Roust the day before came to mind. He had told her that if she left, there was a good chance she couldn't come back. She was a worldwalker, though. As far as she knew, he had never dealt with one before and therefore wouldn't know if that was in fact true.

Ultimately, she decided that if there were any time to try it, now would be it. She had nothing better to do.

She leaned back on the wall and settled in so her body wouldn't come to any harm as she removed her spirit from it. Closing her eyes, she took a deep breath and felt her spirit lift from her body.

After one last glance around, she formed an image of the castle in Pieriun in her mind.

Nothing happened.

Deciding that maybe she wasn't being specific enough, she imagined Eridu's office and tried again.

Still nothing.

Her ability had never failed her like this, not even after she'd first discovered it. Concerned, she decided to see if she could leave in her spirit form without transporting somewhere.

She floated out of the cave and above the trees. Her best guess was that the spell that kept the forges hidden only covered the area where the villages were nestled against the mountain. She looked for the lowest point and flew towards it, picking up speed as she drew near. She had never tested her ability quite like this, but it was fun.

Once she reached that point, she realized she was at the edge of a plateau, and her heart sunk a bit at the view of only more mountains before her. Just as she was about to turn around, a trail carved into the side just below her caught her eye. Deciding that where there is a trail, there must be people, she headed towards it.

A feeling as if she was being pulled backwards made

travel difficult, but she struggled against it, finally breaking free. When she looked back, where she had just been, it looked as if the valley on the plateau was actually the sheer side of a mountain.

Fear struck her. She didn't know what would happen if she stayed away from her body for too long, and her connection to her body was now almost non-existent. She tried to pull herself back to her body, but her spirit didn't move. Moving to where she had previously been, she tried to go through the stone, which she knew couldn't really be there, only to find herself unable to go through it. Odd, considering she could go through literally anything.

This was a mistake. She knew it. The only thing she didn't know was how to fix it.

CHAPTER

FOURTEEN

Adalyn desperately wished that she could use her ability to pull herself to people and not just places. The only person she could think of who may be able to help her was Glenda, and she had no idea where her mentor had gone off to.

But that was not entirely true. Glenda wasn't the only one who could help. Before all of this had started, she had visited Venlian as a spirit. Perhaps he could help. While she didn't know exactly where he was now, she knew that eventually he would head to the guest suite in the castle at Chors.

Taking one last look around to make a mental note of anything that may help her find this spot again, she envisioned the common area of the guest suite and worldwalked there.

She was instantly in a familiar environment. Relief washed through her at the fact that she had been able to worldwalk again.

The room was empty. She checked each of the rooms in the suite only to find them empty, as well.

Movement caught her eye on their balcony. As she moved closer to investigate, the shadow she had seen before moved from the balcony and into the courtyard below. She decided to follow it. No need to worry about hiding herself this time, since whatever it was shouldn't be able to see her in this form anyway. She hurried along as it jumped from shadow to shadow.

Following it out of the courtyard, she noted that every time it appeared, she could see the misty outline of a man. It soon entered a narrow walkway and stood still. Quiet footsteps headed her way, and she turned to find Bevin slipping into the tight space.

A gasp, loud enough that if she wasn't in her spirit form it would have given her away, escaped Adalyn as the dark shadow she had been following became a very solid Nolan.

"Has she turned up?" Bevin asked in a hushed tone.

Nolan shook his head. "We know she went to Pieriun, but she hasn't returned."

"Has she ever done something like this before?"

He shook his head again.

The two stood in silence for a moment.

"I can't help but wonder if part of this is my fault," Nolan said.

"How could it be your fault?"

His voice shrunk. "I've been avoiding her a bit."

Bevin reached for his hand and grabbed his pinky. "Why have you been doing that?"

He looked into her eyes. "After coming here and

spending time with you, my heart is shifting. We weren't really official, but I can't help but worry that I will hurt her."

Laughter erupted from Bevin and quickly turned into a cough. "You must think very highly of yourself to think Adalyn would risk the peace of both kingdoms over you."

"It's not like that. I just," he let out a sigh, "I care about her. I really do, and I will always support her, but I'm really dreading to have this talk with her when she gets back. I don't know how she will take it. I know it sounds lame, but I value her friendship and don't want to lose that."

"I still think that you're a bit full of yourself, but part of what I like about you is that you do care about how your actions affect others. I'm sure that, over time, she will understand."

Adalyn watched them with interest. How natural they seemed together. Her heart twisted a bit at the loss of her first love, but it didn't hurt as much as she had thought it would. Maybe it never really was love, or just a love of a different sort. Truly, if she was so attached to him, it should hurt more. Shouldn't it?

No matter how she felt about this situation, it was uncomfortable to be here in such an intimate moment. She left to return to the guest suite and hopefully find Venlian.

Instead of worldwalking back, she decided to make her way back and keep an eye out for him. She passed a few people, but much to her dismay, never saw Venlian.

Their guest suite was still empty. Adalyn decided that the most likely way to make sure she didn't miss him was to wait in his room. Floating through his closed door, she was surprised to find that it was full of books.

She wandered around the room, glancing at what books would have held her friend's interest so much that he had collected them in piles. They called to her, and it took every ounce of restraint to resist being sucked into them.

The chaos in this room seemed rather out of sorts for how put together Venlian usually was.

Curious what he had been reading most recently, she made her way to the heavy wooden nightstand and was surprised to find a name she recognized: her own. Tempted to allow it to pull her in, she remembered his warning about touching the books of the living, how it could alter or even erase someone in the present. Glancing at the other books on his nightstand, other familiar names jumped out at her. Glenda, King Coeus, Isabella. Why was he pulling so many books here from his library? It seemed unsafe to have them here.

Adalyn turned away from the nightstand to look at the other books in the room, curious if there were other names she'd recognize among them. Venlian suddenly appeared at the foot of his bed, his arms filled with even more books.

"Adalyn!"

She froze. Both his sudden appearance in the room and his reaction to her being there confused her.

Venlian set the books on the bed and hurried over to her. "You're here!" The look of joy shifted into concern. "Not all of you, it seems. What happened?"

"What is all of this, Venlian?" Adalyn gestured to the books in the room.

"When you didn't return, I was worried. I dug into the books of those you may be with to find out what happened to you. You didn't answer my question. Where's your body?"

If she weren't a blue spirit, she was sure her face would be bright red. "I may have ignored the advice of a dragon and explored a little too far in my spirit form."

His eyes glued to her face, Venlian only nodded and waited for her to continue.

"I was taken to the forge master, but he wasn't there. I got curious and ended up outside of their magical barrier, and I can't get back in to return to my body." She watched his face intently, trying to gauge his reaction.

Venlian sat on his bed. "So, you found a forge."

"Rather, it found me, but yes, I found a forge. Two, technically."

"There're quite a few around the world. Rarely does anyone have the opportunity to find more than one, though. I'm surprised it let you in when the forge master was gone."

The thought that there were more than just the two that she'd seen hadn't occurred to her. It made sense, though. Not everyone would be in need of either a bow or a sword.

Adalyn joined him on his bed, or rather, floated above his bed as if sitting on it. It was odd to be around things but not actually feel them. It was not a sensation she was sure she would ever adjust to.

"So… you appeared out of thin air."

"I did."

"Is that your super-secret elf ability?"

Venlian laughed. "Sort of. It's actually an ability that I got when I became keeper of the tomes. I'm connected to the library, so I can jump from it to anywhere I've been or seen previously. I can't jump between places like you can, but it serves me well." The two sat in silence for a moment. "Why are you here, Adalyn?"

"I'm stuck. I don't know where to find Glenda to ask her advice, and you were the only person I could think of who might be able to see me."

"Why don't you know where to find Glenda? Wouldn't she be back at the Capital?"

Adalyn shook her head. "She left to go find someone. It was all incredibly vague."

"So we need to figure this out, then."

"If you don't mind. I could really use your help."

"I can dig through my library and find others with your ability in the past, see if anything like this has happened before. In the meantime, we need a cover story for your absence. It's already been noted by people here, and that could cause an issue with negotiations."

"I was afraid of something like that! What are we going to do?"

He waved her worries aside. "We can tell them you're sick and that I'm treating you. My father knows that I have some healing ability, so he should help encourage them to leave you alone until you're better. It will only buy us a few days at most, though."

"How are the negotiations going?"

"It's frustrating. Every time it seems that we are making progress, at the next meeting we start at square one again."

"What if it's this mistress everyone keeps warning us about?" Adalyn asked. "Didn't Bevin and the golems tell us that she had an effect on the men she's around?"

"They did. I wonder what exactly it is she's doing to them? It could be an enchantment of some kind, but there are other ways to influence people. There are some natural compounds that can either stimulate or dull people's minds…"

"Do you know her?"

Venlian shook his head. "I've never met her. I've only heard of her."

"Maybe I can investigate while in my spirit form and see if I can discover who she is."

"That's a bad idea. There are others with abilities who can possibly see your spirit. I don't know if any of them are here, but if they saw you, it could destroy all chances for peace."

"So, what do I do?"

"I'm not sure. You can wait here while I go back to my library and start swapping these for the other books. Maybe you can help me go through them?"

"I can do that. While you get those, though, I think I'm going to head back to the capital. See if Glenda has returned yet. If not, maybe I can find a spirit to let her know what's happened when she returns."

"What do you mean, if you find a spirit? I thought you told me there were many there."

"They've been leaving. Glenda mentioned it when I last saw her. People all over Pieriun have had abilities manifest, and the spirit who had that ability has been leaving to stay with their partner in ability."

"That's odd."

"Why's that?"

"Only one person at a time has any given ability. There can be similar ones, but there's never been a pair."

"What do you think that means?"

Venlian thought for a moment. "I think the living spell may be behind this. The spirits are still trapped in it, possibly with some connection to their ability still. It does make me wonder…" He trailed off.

Adalyn waited for a few moments in anticipation. "Yes?"

"What if you don't have a full connection to your ability right now? What if Glenda still has part of it?"

CHAPTER FIFTEEN

Adalyn returned to Pieriun and began wandering the halls of the castle, only to be disappointed that the one time she actually needed to find a spirit, she couldn't find any. She had searched the Banneret halls, the tunnels leading up to the castle, and slowly made her way out to the courtyard. Venlian's comment about others being able to possibly see her played through her mind as she made her way to where she hoped she could find Banneret training.

The sound of clashing metal and foul language greeted her as she entered the sparring grounds. She weaved her way through the crowd, waving her arms and trying to be as obvious as she could be. To her dismay, she wasn't noticed.

Standing in the middle of the space, she paused to watch, hoping some sign of which of these men and women were Banneret would become apparent to her. Most were wearing torn-up leathers and fighting with dulled blades, so there was no difference between each person.

Slowly moving among the sparring pairs, she began to feel slight pulls towards certain individuals. Nothing strong like the pull to the books had been, but a feeling of familiarity.

Moving closer to a pair where the feeling felt stronger, she froze as one of the men was hit and flew straight through spirit. A zing of recognition went through her. Family or friend, maybe even companion. No matter what it was, she knew he had to be a Banneret.

She approached him as he pried himself from the heap he had become on the hard dirt ground and reached to let her arm go through his shoulder.

He shivered. "I thought we said no abilities, Craig."

Craig scoffed. "Like I would need my ability to beat you."

The man brushed his own shoulder through her arm still embedded in him. "Seriously, will you stop it?"

Her curiosity peaked, Adalyn removed her hand from his body and continued through the area.

A familiar voice carried over the shouts of the soldiers around her. "Where is your body?"

She turned towards the voice and was relieved to find herself face-to-face with Brinn.

"You can see me?"

"I can."

"How long exactly could you see me for?"

"You've been fading in and out of my vision for a few minutes. I wasn't sure what exactly I was seeing. Flailing arms visible for a moment and gone the next. You would be over there one second and then over there. It wasn't until you stuck your arm in one of your men that you stayed in focus long enough for me to pin you down." Brinn jostled as someone bumped into him. "How about we move somewhere that I'm not going to get beat up?"

She followed him to the edge of the training field, Brinn weaving his way through people. Adalyn decided it wasn't worth the effort. She walked through people as they got in her way, a small feeling of glee filling her at the shivers and surprised looks from unsuspecting soldiers.

Brinn leaned on the gray stone wall and spoke to her while watching the fighting. "What happened to you? I last saw you heading off to clean up from the attack in your village. You disappeared after that. I rode back to the capital to report."

"The forge found me."

He nodded and his body relaxed. "Ah, I see. When the forge calls, we can't refuse it, or we may not receive the opportunity again. You know, King Coeus was furious."

"I'm sure he was. Do you think he will understand if it's explained to him?"

"Perhaps. He still doesn't quite get what we are, but several of his close guards have had abilities manifest. The queen has helped. While she doesn't understand everything about the Banneret, she does have an understanding of those with magical abilities. Some are called to the forges as well. You still haven't answered my first question."

"Oh? I forgot what that was."

"Where's your body? Why are you here as a spirit?"

Adalyn took a few moments to process her answer.

While she was technically his superior, she didn't necessarily feel it and was afraid of his response to her actions.

"I left my body in the barrier around the forge. I explored a little too far and became trapped outside. I don't know how to get back to my body."

Brinn let out a laugh. "You really are just like Glenda. She did the same thing."

"You're kidding me!"

"It's a running joke among the Banneret. I bet you were warned not to try and leave, too, weren't you?"

"Maybe," she muttered.

"Don't worry, just about everyone with your ability has tried it. If you ask her, I'm sure you can find a way back."

"That's just it. I don't know where she is. I was hoping she'd returned here, but I don't see her."

"I haven't seen her either; of course, my ability doesn't quite work like that, either."

"What exactly is your ability? Why can you see me?"

"Communicating and potentially controlling spirits is sort of the base of my ability."

"Really? How so?"

"I can call out to the dead, and they can request a presence with me. When I was young and couldn't control it, I found it overwhelming. The ones who had unfinished business bombarded me night and day. I was nearly driven mad."

"How did you learn to control it?"

Brinn tapped the dagger on his hip.

Adalyn understood immediately. "You found your weapon."

"More like it found me, but yes. It helped keep them at bay until I could control it better."

"No fancy name for your ability? I know mine is worldwalking, and I've heard of a few others in passing."

He shifted uncomfortably and mumbled.

"What was that?"

"I said, necromancer."

"Wait, does that mean you can control more than just the spirits of the dead? You can control their bodies, as well?"

He shrugged. "If I wanted to. I would rather leave the dead at peace."

"Do you think you could use your ability to call Glenda's spirit for me?"

Brinn was silent for a few moments. "Apparently not."

"Aren't you going to at least try?"

"I just did. It didn't work."

"Oh, sorry. Is your ability glitching, maybe?"

"Doubt it. I don't feel off. Of course, she isn't really dead though, is she?"

"How did you know?"

"I may not be the brightest out there, but I do know how the Banneret abilities work and that there's only one person who has it at a time. Somehow she is, but isn't, dead."

Adalyn was disappointed. "Could you see her if she was here?"

"I have before. I could leave my call for her open, sort of like a beacon. While I can't pull her to me, she would see it and potentially come to me when she gets back."

"That would be wonderful. Thank you."

"What are you going to do now?"

"I have a library to visit. Tell Isabella I said hi and that I miss her?"

"Of course."

MAKING HER WAY TO THE LIBRARY WAS ONE OF THE easier worldwalks she had done in a very long time. No barrier to cross, no other people to bring with her, and considering she had done this for years before she even knew she was a worldwalker, it shouldn't surprise her, yet it did.

Venlian stood at a table with piles of books stacked around him.

"I thought you were the keeper of these poor books. What have you done to your library?" Adalyn teased.

Startled, he turned towards her quickly, slamming a book closed in the process. A smile spread across his face as recognition set it.

"I see you made it. I worried you may have forgotten how to get here."

She joined him near the table and skimmed over the titles. "Have you found anything?"

"Not yet. It's hard when I don't know exactly what I'm looking for. I have a few ideas, but that's about it."

"I assume you already pulled the old worldwalker books."

"Should I?"

"They won't necessarily help us with figuring out what's going on with the prince's mistress or figuring out who she is, but it could help me find a way back to my body."

"I don't follow. Glenda's book shows it is complete. We can't find her current location in it."

"True, but apparently worldwalkers have a bad habit of losing their bodies when they go to the forge."

Venlian burst out in a full-bellied laugh. For someone who seemed rather controlled, Adalyn found it nice to hear something so natural come from him.

"Of course, you all would. Let me go pull them out."

Adalyn continued to glance over the titles of the books Venlian had already gathered. A small pull came from all of them, and most had unfamiliar names and symbols on them. The thought crossed her mind that she wished she knew how to help. Anything that would help point Venlian in the right direction to find the mistress would be beneficial.

A sensation of being watched from multiple directions instantly hit her. She spun around, but found no one there. Venlian was back in the aisles out of her sight; the area near her was completely empty.

Picking one sensation, she followed it to a shelf and discovered that it was a book. It seemed absolutely absurd to her that a book would give her the feeling of being watched, but there was no doubt. It had to be coming from this book.

Unable to interact with it, she left to chase down another of the feelings and found another book. A theory began to form in her mind and before hunting down the others, she returned to the table to wait for Venlian.

He had already returned with a stack of familiar

names, many of the same ones she had previously read. Maybe *read* was a bad way to look at it. Perhaps *visited* would be more suitable. She did wonder, because of how she saw the books instead of reading them, if she only saw portions of them and not the entire thing.

"I need to show you something."

Venlian shot her a curious glance. "What do you need to show me?"

"I have no idea, but several books are watching me, and I need you to look at them."

"Excuse me? They're watching you?"

She nodded. "Yeah. I know it sounds odd. It's not the same feeling I get when a book calls to me and pulls me in."

"What do you mean, calls to you and pulls you in?"

Adalyn told Venlian of the books in Chors that she had worldwalked into. A look of concern and curiosity formed on his face as he listened.

"Was this a similar experience to what you did with the books here?"

She nodded.

"Have you ever had any other books call to you?"

"Not that I can recall."

"It's just a theory, but maybe you can do it only with books that are based on truth. Books that have enough history in them for you to somehow connect to it. I'm not entirely sure just how exactly you are getting to view these books with your ability, but I don't think anyone really understands any of the magical abilities fully. Now, about these books that are watching you…"

Adalyn led him to one of the books and Venlian

removed it from the shelf. He glanced quickly at the title, then tucked it under his arm, motioning her to take him to the next one. One after one, they wandered the library, making several trips back to the table, and gathered several large piles of books.

Picking them up individually and sorting them, Venlian spoke. "Curious. These are all from the continent that Chors is on. A wide variety of species, but all from similar timelines. Do you want to see if you can connect with the books I just pulled for you while I look at these others?"

"I can try. They're rather distracting. I can still feel them."

"Do you want to try connecting to the others instead?"

"Do you mind?"

"Go ahead. Why don't you pick one and I will grab another, and we can tag-team this set."

Adalyn skimmed over the pile of books, considering which one she wanted to try worldwalking with. She reached out with her ability to see if one felt different from the others only to find that several had a higher level of interest in her. The feeling was rather unsettling.

A blue leather book with a dragon scale print pressed into it was one of the strongest. This one did feel a bit different, though, vaguely familiar. Not the presence of someone she had spent much time with, but still it seemed to know her somehow.

She reached out her hand and as soon as she connected with the book, a familiar sight unfolded around her.

Tall mountains surrounded her, and a lake with a dam holding it back from a large village stood in front of her. Nearby, a young girl sat crying, cradled in the tail of a large blue dragon—the same dragon who had visited Adalyn in her dream and shown her the devastation of its people.

Adalyn approached the pair and watched as the dragon shifted into a tall, lean woman and scooped the girl up into her arms. “Don’t cry, my little one.”

The girl only cried harder into her shoulder.

“Were they being mean to you again?”

She nodded her head and let out a wail.

“Listen to me. You are a very special dragonling. There are no others like you, and you have a purpose. You just need to be patient enough to discover it.” The soft tones of the dragon’s voice were calming, but didn’t seem to soothe the child.

A strong, rumbling voice from behind her made Adalyn jump. “You are the only child who is a descendent from both of us. A child truly made of love without hatred or prejudice.”

Adalyn watched a ruby red dragon walk past and nuzzle the little girl.

“But I’m hideous!” the little girl said between broken sobs. “I’m not even a dragonling. My skin is pale, and I have no scales. I’m the only child with hair, and I have to wear these coverings to keep myself warm.” She let out a long sob, and a few moments later continued, “I don’t even have a dragon!”

Both dragons allowed her a few minutes to sink into her sorrow before continuing to speak to her.

The blue one broke the silence first. "Do you know why we are here? Have you heard the stories?"

The little girl lifted and shook her head.

"In the world, this," the blue dragon gestured to the girl with the wave, "is what is normal. We are anomalies, feared and thought gruesome, yet hunted for our scales. Most dragon-kind have been killed by now. We take so long to breed and grow to full ages that we were being slaughtered faster than we could reproduce. There are only a handful of dragons left."

The girl wiped a sparkling tear from her cheek. "I don't believe you."

"It's true," the red dragon continued. "We struck a deal with some humans who were able to work magic and created safe havens with them, places where we could train their descendants as well as protect and raise our own. Unfortunately, we were both too old to have our own children by then. The mages used their magic and created children of them and of us, neither fully human nor dragon, something different and unique."

This explained why the dragon who had visited Adalyn in her dream showed itself fully as dragon and the DJs and Makylites appeared more human—because they weren't full dragons. It did make her wonder about what she had seen in the book in Chors with the water dragons, though.

"You, my dear, have something that those other dragons don't." The red dragon wiped the last of the tears from the girl's face with a nuzzle, calm reassurance rolling off him in waves. "These tears show that you have magic, much more than the others here. While they may be able to fly and are strong, you can do many things that they never could."

A small smile emerged on the girl's lips. "I can?"

"You can. You just have to learn how to connect with it."

The loving exchange melted Adalyn's heart, but then she realized that the dragons were still talking, but she could no longer hear them. Her ability or the book had decided that she had seen what she needed to and began to pull her out of the vision in front of her and back towards the library. She traveled through a tunnel of darkness, on the other side of which sat Venlian with his nose deep in a thick green book.

He looked up, his eyes taking a moment to focus, as she reappeared across the table from him. "How did it go?"

"I saw the forge. I don't know why exactly I needed to see it, but I saw two dragons comforting a little girl. I learned a lot of history, but nothing that pointed to anything specifically."

He placed his hand on his book and leaned, stretching his back. "You said you were thinking about looking for the person potentially behind this war, the mistress, when the books felt like they were watching you?"

"Yes."

"What if there were clues to her identity?"

Adalyn moved around the table towards Venlian. "The girl did look human. She was upset that she didn't look like a dragon. She had magical abilities, as well."

He watched as she moved closer. "So, theoretically, she

could be living among the royal family in Chors. What if that little girl was the mistress?"

"Hm. What did you find out?"

"I'm not entirely sure, but this is mostly set in Almendra before it became a haunted wasteland. I'm hoping it will tell me a bit about what happened there."

Adalyn stopped next to Venlian, her hand resting on his arm. The fact that she could feel him, but not the furniture around him, was an oddity she would have to mull over later. The pieces seemed to be falling into place, yet just out of reach of it all to making sense. The scene that had played out before her in another book she had read in Chors came to mind.

She looked into Venlian's eyes. "I wonder if it's the same girl."

"Who is the same girl?" he asked without breaking their gaze. "This book is about a man."

"No, I read, or really, *saw* a woman who knew the queen of Almendra. She had magical abilities, and I watched the city around her turn into monsters tearing each other apart."

A look of confusion crossed his face. "They turned into monsters without anything causing it?"

Adalyn shook her head. "No, I think she was casting a spell of some sort. Smoke billowed out everywhere, and after that, there were only monsters in the city."

Venlian looked back down at the book he had been reading. "I wonder if perhaps they were part of that. I think I may have some disturbing reading ahead of me."

"I can help."

"Are you sure you don't want to look at those?" He nodded to the pile of worldwalker books.

"I feel like this is more important."

The twinkle in his eye and look of concern on Venlian's face made Adalyn's insides twist.

"What?"

He shook his head. "Nothing. If you want to help with these, you are more than welcome. I have a lot to get through."

Realizing that her hand was still on his arm, she pulled it back and reached for another of the books on the table but stopped short. "Venlian? Something isn't right."

"What's wrong?"

"I feel like I'm being pulled the wrong direction."

Venlian stood up and looked her over. "What do you mean?"

"Normally if I'm going to the book to see it, I feel my ability pulling towards the book," she answered, her voice shaking. "Something is pulling me away from it. I can't..."

A ripping sensation ran through her, and she let out a scream as she tried to fight it.

Venlian grabbed hold of her arms and called out Adalyn's name as her spirit began to dissolve from his hold. Her last moment of clarity was of the look of pure terror on his face before darkness took her and her spirit ripped out of his hold.

CHAPTER SIXTEEN

Adalyn awoke with a groan. She felt as if she had just drunkenly fallen out of a second-story window in her old home—somehow completely uninjured, but every single movement filled with regret.

"Let me guess: you're a worldwalker."

Her eyes shot open, and she looked around until she found a stocky, red-scaled man watching her on the other side of a cave. The glow from the forge embers amplified the deep red of his scales and reflected off his pearlescent horns.

Slowly sitting up, Adalyn realized that she was back in her body. She let out a groan. No wonder she hurt so much.

"I am. How did you know?"

"Only worldwalkers give me this sort of trouble," the man said with a chuckle. "Everyone else just hangs around and gets into stuff in my forge. Worldwalkers have a habit of wandering off. I almost always have to bring their spirits back to me. I guess I prefer it this way. Much less mess to clean up after."

What he was saying took a few moments to sink in. "You pulled me back?"

"Of course. I'm the forge master."

"But, how?"

"Nah, I can't give away all of my secrets. You're a bit different though, aren't you? When I pulled your spirit back, your ability felt…" he paused for a moment in thought, "splintered? No. Maybe incomplete? It doesn't really matter. You're here, and we've got work to do either way."

Adalyn couldn't help but feel like this entire situation of worldwalkers wandering off at this forge was a running joke that no one had let her in on. Glenda was going to hear it whenever she found her, because at the very least she should have warned her. While they hadn't seen a lot of each other lately, she was sort of Adalyn's mentor.

The thought of mentors reminded Adalyn of how she had just left Venlian. She was sure he had to be worried about her, but knew there was no way she could get in contact with him. A new sense of purpose and urgency hit her as she focused back on the task at hand.

She stood and stretched her body. The length of time her body had sat here left it stiff. "All right, I'm ready. What do you need me to do?"

He held out his hand. "Let me see your sword."

Adalyn reached over and gave him the sword still in its sheath. He drew it and held it up in the minimal light.

"Do you have your enchantment?"

"My what?"

He lowered the sword and scowled. "Your enchantment. You should have either brought something or gotten an object from the dragonlings below to help strengthen your sword during this process."

Adalyn patted herself down, checking to see if she had anything to offer. Her hand hit a lump in a pouch on her side. She reached in and pulled out the golden scale Roust gave her.

Wide-eyed, the forge master glanced back and forth between the scale and her face. "You convinced a dragon to give you part of their hoard?"

"He rather forced it on me, but yes."

"What exactly did you do for this dragon to have forced you to take part of his hoard?" Waving his hands in front of him, one still holding her sword, he cut off her answer. "You know what? I don't want to know. Not my business. We should get started. The missus will be upset if I'm late for supper, and I know she's making her famous rabbit stew tonight."

He handed her sword back and moved towards the coals. Taking a deep breath in, he blew flames into the furnace hot enough that Adalyn's face felt as if she had stayed out in the sun too long. She quickly raised her hands to cover her face until he was done.

Upon hearing his voice, she lowered her arms. "I've never had someone come in with a piece from a dragon hoard before. This may be interesting."

"Why's that?"

"You saw how they contain their hoards? Ripping out their scales and replacing them?"

She nodded.

"It's a nasty business, but it means that *that*," he pointed to the golden scale still in her hand, "has been attached to other dragons before you were given it. That won't be normal gold. In order for their hoard to stay attached, it literally has to become part of the dragon. That gold will have at least a small part of the essence and possibly physical pieces of the dragon or dragons who wore it before."

Adalyn suddenly felt as if the gold piece in her hand was very dirty. While it shined in the now roaring fire light, she couldn't help but envision bits of dragon attached to this object in her hand. Her stomach turned.

The red-scaled man let out a deep laugh at the disgusted look on her face, "Bring it over here. Let's get you started. I'm Barust, by the way."

Adalyn approached the fire, sword in one hand and golden scale in the other. "Adalyn. What do I do?"

"Place your blade in the flames."

She did as he said, surprised that as soon as it came in contact, the unbearable heat from the fire disappeared and a familiar presence surrounded her. She turned to ask Barust what she needed to do next, but the words never came. An encouraging smile on his face was the last thing she saw before darkness surrounded her.

Turning in a circle, she found herself in a space of nothingness. No boundaries, no light, not even her own body or spirit. Just pure darkness.

"We finally meet," a soft voice reverberated through the space.

Adalyn tried to pinpoint the sound, but still only found the dark.

"Do not worry, you know me. Or at least, we've been together a long time. You may call me Psyche. I am your blade."

Still confused, Adalyn hesitantly attempted to talk. "How can my blade speak?"

"The Banneret weapons are unique. We are not only weapons. When we were created, we were imbued with magic and made sentient beings."

"As a blade?"

"Yes, as a blade."

"Why would they do that? How would they do that?"

"I am not at liberty to discuss my creation, only that I was created to protect and aid those who are gifted the worldwalker ability."

Memories of Venlian and Glenda telling her to keep the blade near floated in front of her, breaking up the darkness. Nolan soon followed as he cut down the death slaugh with her blade after his own did no damage. She finally understood what made her blade able to do things that others couldn't.

The voice spoke over the images as they played without sound in the darkness. "I did not call you to this space only to greet you. It is unusual for us to connect in this sort of way with those we protect, but I am not alone. Another has been alongside you for a while now and wishes to greet you. Will you welcome them into this space?"

Feeling vulnerable, Adalyn hesitated. "Are they safe?"

"That is for you to decide. I would not allow them into this space if I felt they were a threat, though. They have tried to contact you in the past, but you have been unable to hear them."

"I'm assuming that means they aren't an actual physical being."

"You are correct. They are among a world you have yet to visit."

Still wary, but trusting Psyche, she agreed. The memories stopped playing and a small red speck appeared in the distance. Adalyn waited patiently as it grew larger as it came towards her. It seemed that Psyche really had kept this being at quite a distance to protect her.

Recognition struck Adalyn as the figure drew near. The red dragon she had seen in the book with the little girl swooped in and landed in front of her. His claws caused a ripple through the black as it landed on something solid that hadn't been there before.

"It's you!"

The dragon cocked his head, and his rumbling voice echoed through the space. "You know me? I thought I hadn't been able to get your attention."

"I saw you in a book. You and a woman—no, a blue dragon—were comforting a little girl."

"Ah, you saw us with Neith. So you are beginning to understand what I needed to show you."

The name sounded familiar, but Adalyn couldn't quite place where she had heard it before.

"I've seen you two, and your counterpart, the blue dragon, showed me this valley being wiped out by a dam breaking. I don't understand why she needed to show me this."

"That girl learned to fear others as she was raised. She

grew up to be an incredibly powerful witch, but we passed away while she was still very young. We were no longer able to protect or guide her. She became vengeful and obsessed with unlocking her dragon. It was her who caused the dam to break."

A memory wiggled in the back of Adalyn's mind and flickered for a moment in the darkness, but escaped her.

"You said that she wanted to unlock her dragon. Wasn't she a dragonling?"

"She was, but she was born more human than dragon. She did finally succeed. As a teen she became strong enough to break through the barrier and escaped to live among humans. Unlocking her dragon came with severe consequences, though; not only for herself, but for many others."

Adalyn processed everything the dragon was saying, putting together the pieces until suddenly the puzzle formed a complete image. Images flashed through the darkness of the cloaked woman she had watched cast a spell, all living beings around her morphing into monsters. She had left the building before seeing the results of that spell, but Adalyn could only assume that at that moment, Neith's dragon had been unlocked.

Now that she thought about it, there was no question that they were the same person. Those eyes were the same, and ones that she had seen before herself, not just in a book.

"Is Neith the prince of Chors' mistress?"

Adalyn could see a smile pull at the corners of the dragon's mouth. "She is."

All this time, Adalyn had been trying to find the

mistress, to find a way to stop this war, and she had met her—and eaten cake with her—not once, but twice!

"Is there a way to stop her? A way to counter the pheromones? That's how she is manipulating everything, isn't it?"

"Among other methods, but yes. She inherited that ability from me. It's why I needed to find you while you were still here at the forge. There is an herb that is used regularly in the cooking in this valley. Dustbroom is rare and only found in areas such as this. Before you return, you will need to gather as much of it as you can to help counter her effects on the king and his household."

"Where can I find it?"

"Speak to the DJ and Makylites. They will have much of it harvested."

"Thank you. I will do that."

Adalyn watched the dragon as it shifted uncomfortably. She had never imagined a dragon could possibly look bashful, but somehow it did.

The dragon spoke softly. "May I ask you a favor, as well?"

"Of course!"

"Before you leave, will you help the DJ and Makylites? They've always fought, but after our deaths, they became hostile towards each other. They blame the loss of their families on each other and don't know the true reason behind it. Can you share that with them?"

"I will do my best. I can't promise that they will listen."

"I understand. I need to return soon, but I will be with you. As a thank you for helping resolve this, I wish to leave you with a gift. While your mind is here, your body is currently reforging your sword. I no longer have a physical body to give a piece to help strengthen your sword, but I will give you a small piece of my spirit. A part of me will always stay with you, and you can call on me when you need."

Adalyn called out a thank you, but the dragon was already beginning to dissolve into the darkness. She wasn't sure if she had been heard.

Psyche's voice returned once the dragon left. "I see that I will no longer be alone. It's rare that I am able to connect with the worldwalker, but now I will have another to speak with. You are almost finished reforging the sword, and it will be difficult to keep this connection once that has happened. Before we part, I need to tell you that you need to be careful."

"Why is that?"

"You and your Banneret are incomplete in your power. You are all divided as long as the living spell is active. We will meet again when it's time to complete our connection."

Before Adalyn could ask what Psyche meant, Adalyn saw a bright light ahead of her and found herself back in her body, dipping her short sword into a giant container of water. The sudden shift startled her, and her sword fell with a clang as she pulled back and dropped it on the ground.

"Are you all right?" Barust asked, suddenly by her side.

Shocked, Adalyn didn't speak. Instead, she reached down to pick up her sword. It had changed. What had previously been a simple and elegant handle had morphed into a more complex piece. Gold wove through the silver handle, with flecks of blue stone between the swirls, and a brilliant red jewel sat at the top.

"I've never seen a blade reforge quite like this one has. May I?" Barust asked, his hands outstretched.

Adalyn handed the sword to him and watched as he examined it. "Is it usual for the Banneret weapons to speak to their partners?"

The look on Barust's face told her that it was not, in fact, a usual circumstance. "Can you explain what you mean?"

She discussed what had happened while her body was forging the sword. She left out no details.

Barust rotated the sword in his hands again. "That would explain why your sword is so different. I know you're in a hurry, but come back with me to my home for the night. The sun is going down, and we can arrange a meeting with both the DJ and Makylites. This is going to change everything."

CHAPTER SEVENTEEN

"How long have you been a Banneret, Adalyn?"

She ducked out of the way of a branch that Barust had moved out of the way for himself as it flung directly towards her face.

"I'm honestly having trouble keeping track of the time. I guess, for my own timeline, it's been a few months. Pieriun, possibly a year or more. In Chors, only a few days."

The look he gave her over his shoulder said he thought she must be slightly crazy.

Adalyn talked on their way down, telling him of the curse and the issue with the time difference between the two kingdoms. Barust listened and held his questions until after she was done.

"That makes me wonder what happened to the other forges. I know there were many other forges, but if it's been hundreds of years without any Banneret to use them, they may have disappeared. Have you heard of any others still in use?"

"To be completely honest, I'm not sure. I've been so busy trying to take care of this issue with Chors that I haven't been around other Banneret much. I may be in command, but I truly know hardly any of them."

"You're comfortable with that set up?"

Adalyn thought about it for a moment before responding, trying to figure out just how she really felt. "Not really. I've never had interest in being a leader of anything. I'm content with a quiet life. I've already had enough adventure and drama. I went from a good home where I could go to school to homeless and an orphan. I've fought my way back to where I am." Adalyn paused. "Why am I telling you all of this? I barely know you. I just found out your name five minutes ago."

He chuckled. "People tend to do that. It's actually a DJ trait. The parent dragon that we were created from let out a pheromone that caused the opposite sex to relax and be more cooperative. We inherited that ability from them."

The rumors of the mistress crossed her mind, how men were easily swayed to do whatever she wanted them to. "Anything else you inherited?"

Barust veered off the main path and took Adalyn down a much smaller and steeper one. "Short cut," he explained. "Well, we're red and scaly. We are fire resistant and can manipulate it to a degree."

Adalyn's foot slid and she landed hard on her rear, a large cloud of dust billowing up as she made impact with the ground. "Oof! What about the Makylites?"

He offered his hand and helped her back on her feet. "You mean besides being incredibly inflexible know-italls?" He chuckled again, laughing at his own joke. "They're good with nature. The two peoples are a good fit together. Sort of an 'opposites attract' kind of situation."

The book she'd read in Venlian's library that showed a vision of the valley here crossed Adalyn's mind.

"Has a DJ ever coupled with a Makylite?"

"Very rarely. We really don't get along, and it can be... dangerous."

"What do you mean by dangerous?"

"Combining our abilities doesn't always turn out the best eggs. Sometimes they come out... faulty. Or hazardous."

"Have you ever seen that happen yourself?"

"Once."

She waited for him to continue as they swerved around a large boulder, but he never did. She couldn't help but wonder if the little girl she had seen was who he was talking about, or if there was someone or something else.

They continued down the mountain with small bits of chatting along the way. The journey was much shorter than the way up had been, yet still just as exhausting.

Wary eyes followed her as she followed him into the DJ village. She couldn't help but wonder what could have happened for her to be viewed so hostilely among them.

Barust led her to a small stone building with a slate roof, nothing unusual compared to the other buildings she had seen in the village.

As he opened the door, she was immediately tackled by a small dragonling. The hem of her coat caught fire, and she felt the sting of the flame burning her hand as she tried to pat the fire out. Panic took hold as the flames ignored her attempts and continued to eat their way up her clothing.

A chilling splash snapped her out of it, and Adalyn looked up to find a scaled woman holding a bucket above her.

Adalyn found herself unable to look away. "Thank you."

The woman gave her a once over, then hollered at the little dragonling to come back inside.

"Sorry about that. The younglings around here have a mind of their own. Dragons are born a bit feral and grow into their humanity over time."

Adalyn accepted the hand that Barust offered and lifted her soaked self off the hard ground. "Some humans can be a bit feral, as well. No judgement here."

He gave her a look of approval and headed inside. She glanced around to find that they had gathered an audience and quickly followed him in.

The home was simple but lovely. No chairs were in sight; instead, blankets and cushions in bright colors were spread across the space in small piles. She watched as the small dragon that had jumped on her only a moment ago crawled into one of the piles of blankets in a corner and snuggled into a group she assumed were its siblings. Their noses were tucked into their tails as they snuggled up in a huddle.

Barust and the woman sat on cushions at a low metal table in the center of the room. Bowls of stew and warm fluffy bread were set on top.

"Please, join us."

Settling herself in, Adalyn watched as the other two began to eat without saying another word.

Slightly unsettled from the odd behavior, she picked up her spoon and scooped some of the stew. Pausing before putting it in her mouth, she noted an odd smell from the bowl. She looked up to find the other two eating it heartily and decided to take a small taste so as not to offend her hosts.

It took everything in her to not spit out the food immediately. Her stomach revolted at the taste that not only sat in her mouth, but burned her throat and nose. She forced herself to swallow and picked up the bread, hoping that it would ease the anguish of the taste. It, in fact, did not. While it was the lightest and fluffiest bread she had ever encountered, it was incredibly salty.

She glanced around, looking for a drink. Eyeing the pitcher and set of mugs in the center of the table, she poured herself a glass and drank it down so quickly it dribbled down her chin. The thought that it may be disgusting also didn't cross her mind until it was already in her mouth. Thankfully, it was only water.

Setting the mug down, she took a few deep breaths and watched the others eat vigorously.

She tried to think of something to say to break the silence. "You have a lovely home."

The woman paused, a piece of bread still on her lips as she replied, "Thank you."

They continued to eat, and Adalyn glanced around the space, unsure what to say.

"Is it all right if I stay here? I can sleep in the forest if you need. I have plenty of experience. I don't mean to be an inconvenience."

Barust elbowed the woman and nodded in Adalyn's direction. The woman let out a sigh and shot him a dirty look. "Of course not. You are welcome to stay here."

"What my wife means to say is that you are not an inconvenience. It's an honor for us to have you here." He scooped another heaping spoonful of the horrible-tasting stew and shoved it in his mouth.

Adalyn watched the two, still unsure if she should stay. She didn't want to offend them, but they didn't seem to be in agreement about just how much of an intrusion she really was.

"May I ask, did I do something? I noticed the village seemed to feel…" she paused while thinking over the least offensive way to put it, "*uncomfortable* having me here."

Barust elbowed his wife again and shot her a dirty look.

His wife set down her food and let out a sigh while directing a look back at him. "You haven't made us uncomfortable. You were just irregular."

Confused, Adalyn pried, "What do you mean by irregular?"

"Usually when a Banneret comes here, the ward around the valley calls our gatekeeper," the woman explained. "You met her. She was who brought you to my husband's forge. Yet you came from the Makylites. There are rumors that the ward is punishing us and abandoned our gatekeeper."

"You don't need to worry about that. My coming here was manipulated a bit. I wasn't called in the normal sense."

Her eyes narrowed, the woman leaned forward with her elbows on the table. "Explain."

Adalyn shared her experiences since she'd first stepped foot in the valley, how the full dragons had been trying to show her things and what she had been asked to do before she left.

The woman sat there, stunned. "You truly met her?"

"Technically them, but yes. They want for your people to be at peace."

"If a dragon could cry, I would be drowning in tears." The woman reached a hand over and placed it on Adalyn's. "You bring us great news. Finish eating, I will make the arrangements."

AFTER A ROUGH NIGHT SLEEPING WITH SMALL dragons climbing on her, in her clothing, and attempting to sleep on her face, Adalyn found herself in a grove between the two villages the next morning surrounded by dragons. The tension was thick, with Makylites standing on one side while the DJ stood on the other. Neither were being outwardly hostile towards the other, but if looks could kill, this would be a massacre.

Barust and Roust stood on either side of her, silently watching and waiting for their people to fully gather. Once the grove was filled with as many dragons as it could hold, Barust nudged her with his elbow.

She shot him a confused look and shrugged her shoulders.

Roust's elbow dug into her side this time. He nodded

his head towards the gathered dragons. "Let's get this over with before there's blood spilt."

She cleared her throat and squeaked out, "Thank you for coming here today."

The crowd continued to talk amongst themselves.

Roust rolled his eyes and laughed as Barust's booming voice carried over the clearing, "Order! We all have much to do today. The Banneret has something to say."

The crowd quieted, but not without some dirty looks being shot in their direction.

Adalyn fidgeted with her fingers as she tried to gather her courage to speak again. Public speaking had never been one of her strengths.

"Thank you for meeting me here. Some of you know me. You're familiar with Banneret coming to the forge, and I was made aware that my appearance was not done in a typical fashion."

Adalyn shrank as she saw many heads nod and several among the crowd whisper with each other.

"I never meant to cause alarm. While here, I have been shown the hardships that your people have endured, the loss of your parent dragons and of your friends and families."

"Seeing the aftermath and hearing stories isn't the same!" a voice shouted out from the crowd. "You couldn't understand!"

Adalyn was frustrated. "It's more than that, though. I'm a worldwalker," she paused while whispers swept through the crowd, "and they have literally shown me. I *saw* the dam break and flood your villages. I saw the heart-break and devastation."

The crowd fell silent.

"I also saw what—or I should say, who—caused it."

Psyche's voice whispered in Adalyn's mind, "Show them. Use your ability."

"Close your eyes. Let me show you."

After a moment's hesitation while she thought about how exactly to do this, Adalyn closed her own eyes and reached out to feel the aura of everyone in the clearing. She could feel both the red and blue dragon's spirits nearby approaching the clearing.

She attempted to project the images she had seen of the dam breaking and of the little girl. As the dragons' spirits drew near, they aided and added new scenes: Neith begging for help, trying and failing to learn how to control her powers on her own, and becoming vengeful from how she was treated. Her standing at the edge of the dam and magic shooting from her fingertips, shattering the wall that held the water back.

The images cleared and only the two dragons appeared before the crowd.

"Feel us, our children. We are here with you at this moment," the blue dragon said, his voice sending a feeling of calm through the crowd.

"What the worldwalker has shown you is true. Your hatred and distrust has caused your own demise. We have mourned this fall, and if you don't change your ways," the red dragon added with a tone of sharpness in her words, "this will happen again."

"Be at peace, our children. While change is difficult, it will be rewarding. Many of the difficulties that you have experienced can be solved by coming together.

Embrace the differences in yourselves. Do not let us down."

The vision began to dissolve, and Adalyn grew tired. Connecting to this many people for this long and supporting the spirits of two dragons was more than her ability was up for.

Adalyn opened her eyes before any others in the clearing and watched the expressions as everyone else did the same. Many had a look of awe or confusion, while a few had distrust in their eyes.

"How do we know that wasn't a trick?" someone yelled.

"Yeah! If you could show us all that, how do we know that you weren't making it up?" another joined in.

A small chorus of mumbling agreement swept through the crowd.

Adalyn felt the dragon spirits return, but instead of using her to show themselves to their people, their spirits rushed through the individuals with a single word of power.

FOOLS.

She couldn't help but smile as the looks of distrust and anger suddenly shifted to fear. Hers wasn't the only smile. Others in the crowd smirked and smacked the shoulders of those who had previously been cocky and disbelieving.

"Thank you," Barust said, pulling Adalyn's attention away from the crowd.

"I hope it helps."

"It will take time, but you've started stirring their hearts in a way that we never could," Roust added.

Adalyn watched as the crowd began to disperse. "Is there anything else for me to do?"

Barust handed her a small satchel. "You've done more than enough. I imagine that you should be heading back. We rarely leave our mountain, but if you ever have need of us, use this. We will heed the call."

She unwrapped the leather satchel to find an odd object made of red dragon scale. Gilded runes were carved on it, covering both sides. Tucking it into her own bag next to the pouch of dustbroom she had received earlier, she did a quick check that she had everything.

"If you would like, I can escort you out. It would be much faster than you trying to find your own way," Roust offered.

After a last look around and quick farewells, she followed Roust into the forest. A small amount of fear filled her heart with what she was about to do. She had seen the vast power that Neith had and wasn't sure that she could match her, let alone defeat her. While she did feel more powerful since reforging Psyche, she didn't know just what that really meant in an actual fight. The only thing she knew for sure was that if she wanted to ever live her quiet life again, she would have to step up and make it happen herself.

CHAPTER EIGHTEEN

It took Adalyn a moment to decide where to head to first after getting out of the barrier. Roust hadn't returned her to where he'd found her, just escorted her beyond the reach of the spell protecting the dragons. She was tempted to first go to the capital in Pieriun to let Brinn know that she didn't need him to find Glenda anymore, but she had spent most of her energy already. She wasn't sure she had enough left in her to go through the barrier surrounding the continent that Chors was on.

That also left out attempting to get back to Venlian's library. She wasn't sure if he would be there, anyway.

Ultimately, that only left her with one option: heading back to the capital of Chors. She wasn't overly excited about the idea. On top of needing to figure out a way to confront Neith without destroying the chances of peace between the two countries, she also knew that she would see Nolan and Venlian, and those two left her very confused.

Adalyn sat on a large stone to gather herself before

returning. She decided to check everything in her bag and on her person again as she contemplated how to handle everything once she got back, taking advantage of the moment to process while she was still alone.

Placing each item on the grass in front of her, she thought about what she had been through with Nolan—him saving her from the death slaugh, his sneaking into the kitchen to see her, and the two of them training before the capital was attacked.

Placing her wooden plate on the ground, she thought of the two of them dancing at Bevin's sister's wedding, surrounded by candlelight.

As she placed the last item, her tin cup, on the grass, she wondered where her feelings for Nolan had gone. Sure, she still cared for him, but it wasn't like it had been.

Turning to look at the vast landscape laid out below the mountain, the lush green hills broken by shorn cliffs, she wondered if perhaps it was from the time difference. While only days had passed for Nolan, months had for Adalyn. She had been so focused on just getting things done that it had been a very long time since she'd had any actual quality time with him, at least on her end of the relationship.

Remembering that this time she had been stuck in was the same time zone as Chors, she began packing her items back into her bag. A very long time would have passed without her checking in at Pieriun.

As she picked up the plate, an image of Venlian standing near the creek explaining to her why they were being put back together crossed her mind. The golden lines repairing the plates meant so much more to her now that she was actively working on repairing relations between Chors and Pieriun, as well as dealing with the complications from her now much-less-sheltered life.

Gathering herbs with Venlian came to mind as she placed the pouch of dustbroom in her bag. Him mentioning that he had seen he was more than a mere mention in her book had meant so much more than she could have possibly comprehended then.

She suddenly understood.

She understood why she wasn't upset with Bevin and Nolan and was, in fact, quite happy for them.

She understood that her heart had always been at least somewhat attached to someone else. Someone who could see her even in her spirit form, and who she had chosen to visit in her dreams for many years before she even knew she was doing it.

Standing up, she threw her bag over her shoulder and took a final look around, taking in the incredible view that had helped her get a bit of much-needed perspective. With a deep breath, she envisioned her bedroom in Chors and worldwalked away.

Shouts from the sitting room immediately rang in Adalyn's ears as she appeared in her bedroom. Unloading her stuff on the bed, she cracked the door open to see what the commotion was about.

All she could see were golem and human backs towards her, leaning in to see something.

Curious, she opened her door and tiptoed into the room, slowly making her way towards the gathered group.

Their attention was so intent on whatever was in front of them, none of them noticed as she stood directly behind Bevin and Nolan and peeked over their shoulders.

Surprised was an understatement for the view she had before her. Carnelian sat on one side of a table while Lieutenant Vaeren sat on the other. The two seemed to be playing a game Adalyn was unfamiliar with.

"You cheating little sack of bones!" Carnelian shouted, slamming his fist on the table and causing a small pile of stones to jump.

"I-i-it's not my fault that you dwa-a-rves thought it more impo-o-ortant to correct your height ra-a-ather than your bra-a-ins," Lieutenant Vaeren replied with a smirk.

Adalyn knew Lieutenant Vaeren well enough to know that when he got excited his stutter became worse, and seeing the exchange made her smile.

Carnelian's chair groaned as he leaned back and crossed his arms. "What can I say? Bigger is better."

"Says the least smooth golem I've ever met," Adalyn piped in.

The group immediately turned around. A wall of shocked faces surrounded her, and all of them started talking at once.

She held up her hands in front of her as she laughed and stepped back to make a bit of space between them. "One at a time, please! I can't process all of you at the same time."

Lieutenant Vaeren took the opportunity to speak first. "You're a-alive!"

She patted down her body and spun in a circle. "It appears so."

They settled on the furniture as she told them about

everything that had happened. Without thinking, she started to mention the conversation she overheard between Bevin and Nolan, and paused when their faces turned red and they began to squirm in their seats.

"Nolan," Adalyn nodded at him and Bevin, "Bevin. I'm not upset. It took me some time to process, and if we were in different circumstances, I think I would be hurt much more. I care about both of you, though—even consider you to still be friends, if you will have me."

Both of them nodded their heads in agreement, dumbfounded.

She continued with her story, describing everything that had happened at the forge, and waited for the group to respond. The room was silent.

Looking around, Adalyn noticed someone was missing. "Where's Venlian?"

Iolite was the first to speak. "He's been holed up in his room since you disappeared."

Adalyn rose and walked to his door, playing a rhythmic knock on it, only to receive no reply. Concerned, she knocked a second time, with the same result. As she rose her hand for a third, the door flew open, and a slightly disheveled Venlian stood in the doorway. Pure relief and joy crossed his face for a moment at the sight of her.

She squirmed under his gaze and looked down, surprised that she felt so awkward now that she understood where he lay in her heart. "I wanted to let you know that I was back," she mumbled.

Her eyes slowly rose to his face. He only gave her a gentle nod.

Her face on fire, she quickly turned from him towards their audience, at which they all suddenly found various random objects in the room overly fascinating.

Folding her hands in front of her and quickly walking to join the larger group, she regained their attention. "So! Who has an idea of how we can get the men in the castle to ingest dustbroom?"

Now that an escort of soldiers was surrounding her, Adalyn's nerves were getting the better of her. Sure, the idea of requesting an audience with the queen, filling her in on everything she had learned, and asking for her assistance had sounded like their best option a few moments ago, but was it really?

She could be accused of trying to poison the royal family. Or of flat-out lying to them and making it all up. Both seemed very likely possibilities in her mind, ones that grew more likely with each step she took towards the queen's apartments.

She shifted the bag of books on her shoulder, the only physical evidence she really had to prove her case.

They paused in front of the queen's apartment to be announced.

Then Adalyn took a deep breath and took her first step towards either the best or worst decision she had ever made.

Queen Faith sat at a table with a variety of delectable treats in front of her. Her emerald-green skirt flared out around her, every bit of her perfect.

"Come in, Adalyn. Please join me." The queen gestured with her hand in the smallest of ways toward the other chair at the table.

Adalyn slowly approached the queen and sketched a small bow before setting the bag down and accepting the chair that had been offered.

A warm smile spread across Queen Faith's face. "What brings you to requesting my presence on this lovely day?"

Glancing around to see just how many guards were in the room, Adalyn replied quietly, "I have something of a very delicate nature to speak to you about. I'm afraid it would be best if heard by as few ears as possible, particularly those of the opposite gender. It is in relation to what we discussed during our last tea."

An understanding look crossed the queen's face, and she motioned for all but her maid to give them privacy.

"You may proceed."

Adalyn began to take books out of her bag and place them on the table as she explained what she had discovered.

The queen listened without giving anything away emotionally. "You would stake your life on this intelligence you are giving me?"

"Yes, I absolutely would. It isn't just your kingdom that is in danger. It's many."

"So, my son's mistress is really a dragon and truly is the one behind this war. I wondered how she had woven her way into his heart so quickly, as well as the hearts and minds of most of those in the castle. Do you have a way to stop this?"

Adalyn pulled out the bag of dustbroom and placed it on top of the books. "This is where I need your help."

Queen Faith eyed the bag. "What exactly do you need me to do?"

"Take this and make it into a tea, broth, ale… anything that will have the men in this castle ingest it. It will counter her pheromones and should release them from her spell."

"How do I know that you aren't trying to poison us?"

Knowing that this question would come up didn't help Adalyn dread it any less. "I wouldn't be suggesting only the men in the castle take it if I intended to kill you all. If you really need it, you are welcome to have me test it first, at any time of your choosing so you know there's no antidote taken beforehand."

The queen smiled and winked at her. "I may not have known you long, but I do trust you. Let's just say it's women's intuition."

Unsure just how much to read into that statement, Adalyn chose silence instead.

"I will arrange for a grand council followed by a meeting with you and your people tomorrow. I'll give the king, my son, and their council this," the queen gestured towards the dustbroom, "in every bit of food and drink provided at their meeting beforehand. I don't want to risk it wearing off before we've had the opportunity to see how well it works."

Adalyn was both relieved and a bit afraid. "Is there anything I should prepare my people for with this meeting tomorrow?"

"Nothing in particular. I will make sure to attend and

request your entire group to come with you. That includes those golems."

"How did you…"

"Know about the golems? Ever since you became sick, they spent almost all of their time in your guest suite."

"Oh. You're not offended?"

"Not at all. I've got a very good read on people, and I'm familiar with one of your golems personally from my younger days. It actually made me trust you even more because of your connection to them. Would you like a cucumber sandwich?"

Queen Faith motioned towards one of the towers of snacks on the table.

So engrossed in the task at hand, Adalyn had forgotten that there was food and drink there. She collected a small assortment of treats and sandwiches and prepared her tea in a delicately painted cup with ivy leaves and gold trim.

"Yes, thank you." Adalyn let out a deep sigh of relief, gaining a reassuring nod from the queen.

"Make sure to get some rest tonight. Tomorrow will be a very big day, even bigger than you realize."

Queen Faith's mischievous grin and tapping fingers made Adalyn's stomach twist.

"How so?"

"I'm sending a summons to Neith to participate in this, as well. I want to see her face as everything she's done all falls apart."

CHAPTER NINETEEN

The stomping of their group and guards as they walked down the maze of stone hallways towards the throne room helped calm Adalyn's nerves a little. She hadn't slept much the night before, with all of the potential scenarios of today's events playing through her head.

Bevin sent a reassuring smile as Adalyn glanced at her from her left. While she wasn't technically part of their party, she had been approved as a trainee soldier to be part of their escort and guard in the throne room.

Meeting eye-to-eye with everyone as the double doors began to loom over them felt like a pact was being made between them. Everyone felt the weight of this moment, the potential catastrophic consequences that it could have on millions of lives if it went wrong, and there was no scenario where this would be an uneventful meeting.

All too quickly, the massive doors stood directly in front of them and groaned as they parted. Adalyn straightened her coat she stepped through.

The room was more crowded than when she had seen it before. The king sat on his throne, with Queen Faith on one side and his son on the other. Zephyr stood just behind the king's throne, and the edges of the room were filled with advisors and members of the upper court muttering amongst themselves.

Adalyn and Queen Faith's eyes met, and a small nod from the Queen told her that it had been done.

The group made their way up to the thrones and bowed.

"I see you've made it," King Garren waved his arm towards the group, "and made a few friends while you were here."

Adalyn's gut twisted. Should she tell him that they've known each other all along?

"Yes, they are good friends of ours. We met them in Pieriun just before traveling here," Venlian said, making the decision for her.

The king eyed them. "Why was this not mentioned before?"

"Your majesty, it never came up in our brief moments of conversation. Our time was usually engaged in more important matters," Venlian replied again.

Adalyn was relieved that he had taken the lead. She was too nervous to feel comfortable in that role.

King Garren glanced back at Zephyr, who nodded in return. He cleared his throat. "I see. I do wish that you had told me, though," he looked at the golems, "that any of you had told me."

"Wouldn't have made a difference either way," Carnelian grumbled quietly.

"What was that?" Queen Faith asked.

"Please excuse him. He's a bit out of sorts," Lazuli quickly replied.

"Says who? I'm no different than I was yesterday, or the day before. Can we get on with this? I don't have all d—"

Carnelian went silent.

Adalyn turned to look and found him frozen in place. Confused, she took a few steps towards him to find Lieutenant Vaeren standing behind the rocky giant, holding Carnelian's keystone.

Eyes wide and his whole body shaking, Vaeren's eyes darted among their party as if asking for help.

Venlian stepped forward and gently removed the keystone from his trembling hands. "Why don't I take that? Just to make sure it doesn't get dropped."

Vaeren nodded and handed it to him. "C-couldn't let his a-a-attitude affect n-n-neg-otiations," he said, stepping away from Carnelian as quickly as he could, almost tripping over his own feet in the process.

A flicker of amusement on the king's face put Adalyn at ease. At least he didn't seem to be upset with the outburst.

The groan of the large double doors made everyone turn towards them.

A billow of layers of blood-red silk made Neith's entrance quite dramatic. It was the opposite of the attire Adalyn was familiar with her nighttime cake-eating companion usually wearing. Neith's hair was piled on her head with ringlets falling down her back and ruby pins holding the curls in place. Everything about her said confidence and power.

Adalyn moved quickly to the side, as did the rest of her party, to make way for Neith to pass them.

With a swoosh of her skirts, Neith bowed before the King and joined the prince by his side. She wore a confident smile as she looked down her nose at those around her.

"Let's begin." King Garren announced. The room immediately grew silent. "I have come to a decision about our war with Pieriun. After much deliberation, I have decided that we will officially stop our attacks on Pieriun and enter into a truce."

Whispers spread around the room again. Adalyn glanced at Neith, who did not look very happy.

"Furthermore," the king continued, causing the room to silence again, "it has been brought to my attention that this situation has been manipulated. Our kingdom has suffered heavy losses because of the actions of another."

Gasps and cries of outrage rose from those around the room.

Neith looked quickly at the king and glanced around the room at the reactions.

"I will not let this individual influence our kingdom any longer. This person will be taken prisoner and executed." King Garren turned to Neith. "Guards, detain my son's mistress, Neith."

"How dare you!" Neith screamed as she lunged for the king.

Drawing her sword in an instant, Adalyn worldwalked to block the King from the attack. She bashed the hilt of her sword into Neith's face, causing blood to spray from her nose.

Neith stumbled back a few steps before finding her footing.

"*You!* How dare you get in my way!" Neith's voice grew deeper as she spoke. Her body began to grow, and the fabric of her dress ripped to reveal scales forming on her skin.

"She's shifting!" Nolan shouted. "Everyone get back!"

Glancing around the small room as Neith grew, Adalyn realized that a fire breathing dragon in this room would either burn or crush everyone in here in an instant. Her gaze connected with Venlian's. As if he could read her mind, his eyes begged her not to do it.

She closed her eyes for a moment, took a deep breath, sent the best apology look she could to him, and ran towards Neith. As soon as she came in contact with her, she worldwalked them to a large, forested area.

Now a full dragon, Neith roared and swatted Adalyn off of her.

Adalyn was smacked several feet up into a large tree and dropped to the ground. She groaned as she picked up her sword again and faced the beast before her.

Neith began circling, her large body somehow deftly weaving in and out of the trees. "You did this to me, didn't you?"

Adalyn spun to keep Neith in her line of sight. "I was part of it, yes."

Smoke curled from the dragon's nose. "You, insignificant little thing, thought to stop me?"

Adalyn dove as flames blew past her and hit the tree

she had been in front of only a moment before. Sunlight reflected off deep purple scales as it peeked through the leaves above them.

Adalyn watched and took in their surroundings. She had chosen a random area of forest that she had only walked through on their way to King Garren. If she remembered correctly, it was far away from any village or city.

Her sword in her hand, Adalyn shifted on her feet, gathering the nerve to charge. As soon as the dragon entered an area with a tight gathering of trees that would prevent her from dodging, Adalyn worldwalked above Neith. She yelled as she slammed her sword down with both hands.

The sword glanced off the scales, and Adalyn slid off as Neith slammed into a row of trees in an attempt to crush her.

Panting from the hard fall, Adalyn looked for another opportunity to strike. "I can't let you continue to destroy kingdoms for no reason."

Neith released a wicked chuckle. "Who said it was for no reason?"

"There's never a good reason to start a war."

"No? You wouldn't understand even if I did explain. You're not worth my time."

Adalyn backed up as Neith stalked towards her.

More smoke curled from the beast's nose, and a predatory snarl rolled from her lips. "You are nothing. A no-one who is only a blip in time, while I am eternal."

"You're not eternal. I know much more about you than you realize."

"Oh? I highly doubt that."

Keeping the dragon towards her front, Adalyn weaved between trees as she watched for her next opportunity to strike.

"I know you aren't a full dragon. Your people mistreated you, and yet you became strong and eventually left them."

A look of surprise flashed across Neith's face for only a moment before she crouched lower and hastened her pacing.

"Ah, so you have been to the forge. The Banneret always were pests, appearing just long enough to get in our way and never contributing for the help we rendered them."

Adalyn filed that away as a problem to solve later. She hated to admit it, but there was a good chance Neith was right. She didn't know how to solve it yet, since it seemed that Banneret had no control over when they were called to a forge, but that was a problem for future Adalyn to solve. If there was going to be a future Adalyn. At the moment, she wasn't very confident in that possibility.

"You did escape, though. You had the chance to have a new life, and I don't understand why you turned away from the one you created. I saw you with the queen of Almendra. You seemed to be in her service. Why did you turn against them?"

Neith leapt forward and swatted at Adalyn with her large claws. Adalyn worldwalked a short way to the side. She didn't dare jump behind herself, since she didn't know what was there.

"You're a quick one, aren't you, worldwalker? Should

have figured." Neith quickly redirected and followed Adalyn. "I never turned against them. They took me in and treated me as family."

"So why did you turn them all into monsters, then? Why did you curse them?"

Something caught Neith's eye, and before Adalyn could turn to look to see what it was, she tripped over a branch and fell backwards. Neith flew over the top of her and burst into open sky, her wings spread wide. Adalyn watched as her claws narrowly missed grabbing her as she landed on her back and tumbled down a steep hill. Her head hit a rock as she rolled down, and her vision swam.

Over and over she rolled, until claws wrapped around her, and suddenly she found herself being lifted into the sky. She tried to worldwalk, but couldn't think straight. The throbbing in her head was too much.

"You truly think I wanted to curse the only people who ever treated me decently? It was an accident. When I finally set my dragon free, the spell backfired. It not only set my inner beast free, but did so with all others around me."

Trying not to vomit, Adalyn yelled up at her captor, "An entire kingdom, though?!"

Neith shook Adalyn's body and pumped her wings to push them even higher. "I had no control over how far the spell went! I didn't know that would happen!"

"Why didn't you fix it?"

"I tried, but people like you started nosing around and turning on me. My beast began to get hungry. Not just for food, but the magical energy of others. Do you know how much magic is wasted on battlefields? Spells cast against one another, and only a tiny fraction of their power ever actually hits the intended target. A much less messy way to feed her than just sucking mages dry, don't you think?"

Adalyn opened her eyes and looked down only to immediately shut them again. The trees below her looked the size of grains of rice. She tried to worldwalk again, only to have the nausea hit her once more.

"You know this is wrong, Neith!"

"What I know is that you just cost a lot of people their lives by butting into my business. They will all be on your shoulders! The funny thing is, you may not even be around to see it."

Adalyn felt her magical energy begin to leave her body. She screamed in agony as Neith began to feed on it.

"Hmmm, I've never tasted a worldwalker before. You're so… eclectic."

Unwilling to let the short reprieve while Neith spoke pass her by, Adalyn tried to worldwalk again, only to flicker away for a moment and come back midair in the same spot. Neith had already flown higher, so no claws caught her. Her body immediately began to fall.

She heard a roar as Neith realized that she had lost her.

Adalyn's body gained speed quickly as she fell through the sky. She called on her ability repeatedly, only for it to sputter and fail.

Looking up, she saw Neith closing the distance between them.

Panic set in. She needed an escape.

Adalyn closed her eyes and called out with her ability again, willing her body to worldwalk. She didn't care where she ended up, as long as it wasn't splattered on the ground ahead of her. She was sure that would be the case once Neith drained her of her ability if she was caught.

Her body slammed onto something hard, and the air left her lungs. Adalyn cried out with what was left; a few things seemed to have broken with the hit.

She opened her eyes but saw nothing. Closing and opening them again made no difference. Lifting her arms in front of her, they moved only a few inches before they hit something solid. Ignoring the pain, she wiggled around and found that she was in a very small, dark space.

Calling on her ability to escape, she screamed again, this time in frustration.

She was trapped.

EPILOGUE

NEITH'S JOURNAL

23rd Moon of the 42nd Cycle of the Red Crest

I'm free! After 109 years being trapped with and ridiculed by my fellow Makylites and DJs, I am finally free! Those sorry good-for-nothing dragons can keep their stifling and boring society. Who knew winged beings would be so accepting of being trapped in a valley when they could be free?

I will never return. I don't know where I will go or how I will release my own dragon, but I swear I will. I have magic and am not weak. I refuse to be weak or pitied. My dragon does, as well.

27th Moon of the 42nd Cycle of the Red Crest

This swamp can go to Frishta for all I care. Why did I go this way? I knew we were at the top of the mountain and had to choose a side to climb down. The cloud coverage was so thick I couldn't see a difference between the two, but I am sure that the other one would have been better. It has to be.

The mosquitos are so thick I constantly have them fly into my mouth. If it wasn't for my thick skin, one of the only things I inherited from my dragon side, I would be riddled with bites. Fortunately, the swamp is full of creatures, so my belly is never empty, even if the water is rank and thick.

Last night I was tempted to turn around, but the daunting task of climbing the mountain only to have to scale the other side back down is just too much. I thought when I was free of the valley my suffering would be over, but this is just suffering of another name. Perhaps I can get a few hours of sleep and get out of this forsaken swamp soon.

13TH MOON OF THE 43 CYCLE OF THE RED CREST

It's perfect! I knew I needed to find a way to have access to tools to test my spells, and heard of an opening in Almendra's royal court for a healer. They aren't afraid of magic, and with their funding, I could gain access to what I need to break my dragon free. Now to just find somewhere to work outside of the castle where I won't be noticed.

6TH MOON OF THE 45TH CYCLE OF THE RED CREST

What did I do?! It worked, but it didn't… or it did,

but I messed it all up. They're gone. All of them are gone! Well, not really. They're still here. They just aren't them anymore.

My dragon is content, at least. Everyone has become a beast like she is. I have to get this under control before everything is lost. I must get my dragon back under control. She always demands more and more, and I don't know how to stop her. I left the capital days ago, and everywhere has been affected. There are no beings below, only beasts and the carcasses of the weaker ones. I'm returning to the mountain. With wings, I can fly over instead of climbing. Perhaps the other side hasn't been affected yet.

I don't want to be alone. I have my dragon, but she is a bit mad, and if I'm left with only her, soon I will be mad, as well. The other dragons never mentioned their dragons being split from them as if they were a separate being. What is wrong with me?

What's Next?

Can't wait to read the final book in the series? Follow along as I publish this on Kindle Vella. I've teamed up with my editor and it is being edited as I write it. You can find Paragon's Vella on my Amazon Author profile along with all of my other books. If you aren't a fan of Kindle Vella, Paragon will be released in early 2023.

https://www.amazon.com/Jamie-Dalton/e/B09FGKZMBX

If you've really enjoyed this book help me spread the word! A review is an author's bread and butter and how many readers decide if they will give a new to them author a chance. Feel free to follow me on any of the platforms as well to know when new books are released. It's also how many authors decide which book series to work on next.

Amazon:
https://www.amazon.com/gp/product/B09RK14X5K/

Goodreads: https://www.goodreads.com/book/show/60496013-dragonborn
Bookbub: https://www.bookbub.com/books/dragonborn-the-banneret-series-book-2-by-jamie-dalton

JOIN MY NEWSLETTER & GET A BOOK FOR FREE!

Join my newsletter and get a free copy of The Black-Backed Mirror. A dark fantasy prequel to my retelling series that releases in December 2023 with Throne of Slumber.

https://BookHip.com/STGVCDQ

THE BLACK-BACKED MIRROR

They said if you looked in a black-backed mirror on the stroke of midnight during the full moon that you would see your true love or your demise.

Claire had had enough of letting fate control her life. She swore never to be a slave to anyone or anything ever again. A black-backed mirror was the last thing she was interested in. At least until an unusual wizard appeared with the opportunity of a lifetime

Crème Brûlée

6 egg yolks
2 cups whipping cream
1/3 cup granulated sugar
1 teaspoon vanilla
Boiling water
8 teaspoons granulated sugar

Heat oven to 350°F. In 13x9-inch pan, place 4 (6-oz) ceramic ramekins. In small bowl, beat egg yolks gently. In large bowl, stir whipping cream, 1/3 cup granulated sugar and the vanilla until combined. Add egg yolks; beat with whisk until thoroughly combined. Pour cream mixture evenly into ramekins. Gently place pan with ramekins in oven. Pour boiling water into pan to reach 2/3 the height of the ramekins.
Bake 30 to 40 minutes or until top is light golden brown and sides are set. The center should have a bit of jiggle.
Carefully transfer ramekins to cooling rack from pan while hot. Cool to room temperature. Cover with plastic wrap and chill 4-48 hours.
When ready to use, remove plastic wrap and blot any moisture on the top with a papertowel. Sprinkle 2 teaspoons granulated sugar over each ramekin.
Baby dradon or kitchen torch option: Hold 3-4 inches from custard and move in a circular motion until the sugar is braown and melted. About 2 minutes.
Oven broiler option: Turn your oven to broil. Sprinkle 2 teaspoons brown sugar over each ramekin. Place ramekins in a cookie sheet with sides. Broil with tops 4 to 6 inches from heat 5 to 6 minutes or until brown sugar is melted and forms a glaze.

One Mug Chocolate CAke

¼ cup all-purpose flour
¼ cup white sugar
2 tablespoons unsweetened cocoa powder
1/8 teaspoon baking soda
1/8 teaspoon salt
3 tablespoons milk
2 tablespoons canola oil
1 tablespoon water
¼ teaspoon vanilla extract

Mix all ingredients into a large mug or small soup bowl. If you use too small of one it will spill over as it cooks.
Microwave until done in the middle around one minute fourty five seconds.
Eat while reading a good book.

ACKNOWLEDGMENTS

Thank you so much for taking the time to follow Adalyn's journey. Hers was a story that began as two different books and after scrapping both of them melded into a unique fantasy world with a girl who just wants to be able to live a quiet life.

To my beta readers and ARC readers, you are seriously the best. This book became what it is because you have been there for me. Sometimes when I completely doubted myself.

To my husband, Andrew. Thank you for supporting me on this author journey. For encouraging me, giving me ideas, and helping me find the time to make this happen. I appreciate you so much.

To my daughter, Cassie. These books that I write are my inheritance for you. When your father and I are gone I may not have much to give but these worlds that I hope you can escape into when you need a break.

To Jenny, This book almost didn't release. Life got tough and you told me that you would support me no matter what and help make this happen. It's crazy to see how quickly things can turn around and you were a big part of me pushing forward.

To Clara, thank you for helping keep me sane. For the incredible formatting that you do for me and for being so supportive. I love our late-night talks and having a book buddy to bounce stuff off of.

Alexis, Trish, Elle, and Logan… you are the best author support group. Just thank you.

To DJ and Makyla. Thank you for letting me take a random teasing conversation between you two and turn it into an entire society of dragons.

ABOUT THE AUTHOR

Jamie Dalton is an author of YA fantasy. Growing up in Oregon and Idaho she fell in love with the magic of the mystery of the forests and history. After moving to North Carolina with her husband, her sass took on a life of its own and sassy magical fantasy stories began to be written. She fell in love with the publishing world and became a book cover designer as well as an author which she does during the night while her toddler sleeps. After all, it's called the witching hour for a reason.

If you do like her, (and I really hope you do!) you can follow her anywhere and everywhere.

Author website: Home | Author Jamie Dalton
Facebook author page: Log In or Sign Up to View
TikTok: Magnetra (@magnetra) TikTok | Watch Magnetra's Newest TikTok Videos
Amazon profile: Jamie Dalton
Newsletter: Sign up
GoodReads: Reviews and purchase
Universal Purchase link for non US readers